BLONDE BAIT

"...a twisty, nasty noir."
 –Ed Gorman

"...taut understatement of violence and sex.."
 –Anthony Boucher, *New York Times*

"...most accomplished…"
 —Bill Pronzini, *Mystery*File*

"…all the earmarks of good pulp."
 —*GoodReads*

BLONDE BAIT
by Stephen Marlowe

Black Gat Books • Eureka California

BLONDE BAIT

Published by Black Gat Books
A division of Stark House Press
1315 H Street
Eureka, CA 95501, USA
griffinskye3@sbcglobal.net
www.starkhousepress.com

BLONDE BAIT
Published by Avon Publications, Inc., New York,
and copyright © 1959 by Stephen Marlowe.

All rights reserved under International
and Pan-American Copyright Conventions.

ISBN: 979-8-88601-032-9

Text design by Mark Shepard, shepgraphics.com
Cover design by Jeff Vorzimmer, ¡caliente!design, Austin, Texas
Cover art by Ernest Chiriacka
Proofreading by Bill Kelly

PUBLISHER'S NOTE:
This is a work of fiction. Names, characters, places and
incidents are either the products of the author's imagination or
used fictionally, and any resemblance to actual persons, living
or dead, events or locales, is entirely coincidental.
Without limiting the rights under copyright reserved above, no
part of this publication may be reproduced, stored, or
introduced into a retrieval system or transmitted in any form
or by any means (electronic, mechanical, photocopying,
recording or otherwise) without the prior written permission of
both the copyright owner and the above publisher of the book.

First Stark House Press/Black Gat Edition: June 2023

CHAPTER ONE

It started to snow again a few minutes before I pulled the bus up in front of the hotel, fat wet flakes falling heavily, without any wind, from a sky the color of slate. I shut the motor, yanked the door lever and took my skis out of the bus, then waited on the shoveled sidewalk while the members of the morning class filed from the bus with their skis on their shoulders.

I stacked my skis and poles in the garage and went in the front entrance of the hotel, stomping the snow off my boots on the doormat. The lobby was crowded because it was almost time for lunch. Elaine Skinner, the Whiteface social hostess, caught my eye right away. She came over. "You're just in time, Chuck," she said, not smiling.

"What's the matter?"

"Mr. Rowe and Jack McCall. I think Mr. Rowe fired him."

"Again?" I said.

"This time it's serious."

"Where are they?"

"Mr. Rowe's office."

I walked across the lobby, smiling and nodding when the guests smiled and nodded at me, and went into the manager's office without knocking.

"Two weeks' pay?" Kirby Rowe was saying angrily. "I wouldn't give you taxi fare to the station. You're lucky I don't call the cops on you." His eyes flicked toward me. "Keep out of it, Chuck."

I lit a cigarette and shut the door behind me. "What seems to be the trouble?"

"Ah, this guy," Jack McCall said sullenly. "If he don't

fire me, I'm quitting."

McCall was a cocky Irish kid with freckles and red hair. He'd signed up with the Hotel Whiteface at the beginning of the winter season. Two teams of huskies came with him. As far as I knew, they were the only huskies in the Adirondacks and Jack McCall, who came from Alaska, was the only one who could handle them. The huskies were pretty important at the Whiteface, for next to skiing, Jack McCall's dogsled rides were our biggest winter attraction.

"He hasn't fired you and you're not quitting," I said. "You signed up for the season, Jack. Now, what's the matter?"

"I caught him making a pass at one of the guests," Kirby Rowe said.

Last week it had been gambling. McCall had taken four college kids for a hundred bucks in a game of pot-limit red-dog.

Kirby Rowe had fired him then and I had rehired him.

"Jack?" I said.

"I thought she was asking for it. I thought she was practically begging for it. Maybe I made a mistake."

"He's lucky I don't call the cops on him," Kirby Rowe said.

"She holler?"

"No," Kirby Rowe admitted. "I found them in the hall."

"He's all the time snooping around," McCall said.

"Who is she?"

"Mrs. Kemp in 305," Kirby Rowe said.

Mrs. Kemp. For a moment I thought of an irate husband and a rumpus down at the sheriff's substation, but then I remembered that 305 was a single room and that Mrs. Kemp had it all to herself.

"You're still on the payroll," I told McCall. "I'll see Mrs. Kemp. We'll leave it up to her. Meanwhile, act like nothing's happened. You better get the afternoon sled list from Elaine."

"I don't know," McCall said.

"I do know! Go on, get back to work, Jack."

McCall looked at me and at Kirby Rowe, and left the office.

Kirby Rowe said, "One of these days you're going to remember, Chuck."

"Remember what?"

"The sign on the door. It says 'manager.'"

"You want to make an issue out of that, it's all right with me."

Kirby Rowe's lips tightened. He was a tall man with very black hair graying at the temples. He had a trim moustache that he habitually worried with his index finger. He wore banker's gray most of the time and a black knit tie you'd need a pair of pliers to unknot. He said, "Hadn't you better ask Mrs. Cameron before you see the Kemp woman?"

Mrs. Cameron owned the Whiteface Hotel. She was also my wife, but my name is Odlum. Everyone called her Mrs. Cameron and they called me Chuck. After the honeymoon last year Kirby Rowe had started that and it had stuck. That was one of the things between us.

All I said was, "I'll take care of it." Then I went out to the lobby. I called 305 on one of the house phones but got no answer. Well, Mrs. Kemp could keep till later. I remembered her vaguely as a small but stacked blonde who'd run up a man-sized bill at the bar and who didn't socialize much.

I clomped upstairs in my ski boots and let myself into our room with my key. Inez lay on the bed in her bra and panties. Her long firm limbs were bronzed and slick with suntan oil. The plastic cups over her eyes were staring up sightlessly at the sun lamp and her lips were parted slightly. Even in winter Inez had to have her sun.

"How'd it go this morning, Chuck?" she asked in her throaty voice. "Any casualties?"

"Not a one. Pretty good skiing. Twelve-inch base with a couple of inches of powder."

Inez sat up and the plastic cups fell off her eyes. "You can turn it off," she said.

I shut off the sun lamp, sat down on the edge of the bed and started to unlace my ski boots. Inez unfastened her bra and turned over on her belly. She said, "Give me a back massage, Chuck."

She didn't ask for it, she told me. That was one of the little things about Inez. She never had any questions for anyone, except the rhetorical ones like how'd it go this morning; she just told you what she wanted. She was Inez Cameron, wasn't she?

I straddled her buttocks and began to knead the smooth, flat muscles of her back, working the firm flesh around her shoulder blades and at the base of her neck.

"No, down along the spine."

She crossed her arms on the pillow and turned her face sideways on them. Her eyes were shut, but not squinched shut. She sighed as I ran my thumbs down the delicate vertebrae ridges on either side of her spine.

"Stiff as a board all morning," she said. "Louis threw another one of his temper tantrums." Louis was the pastry chef. "Ah, that's better, Chuck. Right there."

Often, a back massage was a prelude to love-making between us. I felt the stirring of desire and hated myself for it.

Inez didn't like to make love in daylight; in a year of marriage she'd made that clear.

"All right, that's enough." Inez lifted her head and smiled over her shoulder at me.

I ran a finger lightly along the side of her breast, but she let her head drop back to her crossed arms quickly. She had long brown hair with glints of red in it. She was one of those tall statuesque brunettes, about five-eight barefoot. With those long, smooth curves stretched out on the bed she could take your breath away and drop it somewhere in the next county.

I made a half-hearted effort to grab her shoulders and turn her over, but she lay there stiffly. "Not now, Chuck, please," she said. "I have to take a shower and put my hair up and look patrician for the guests."

Sitting on the edge of the bed again, I took off my boots. "Speaking of which, Jack McCall made a pass at one of them."

"Oh, my. I'll bet Kirby was furious."

"Almost blew his stack. I think I can pick up the pieces, though."

"One of these days you'll get Kirby really mad, Chuck."

"Yeah? So what?"

"We couldn't get a better general manager."

"We couldn't get another team of huskies."

"You don't like Kirby, do you?"

"Well, you won't catch us holding hands on off-duty hours."

"Is that supposed to be a crack?"

"I said it. You make it anything you want."

"What was between me and Kirby is finished."

"All right. Swell."

"... Chuck?"

"I didn't go anyplace."

"Why do we always have to argue? I didn't marry Kirby. I married you."

"That's right, Mrs. Cameron."

"Odlum. I'm Mrs. Chuck Odlum."

"Then tell Kirby. I know it."

"Well, aren't we sensitive today!"

"Forget it."

"I don't want to forget it. You're making an issue out of it. Owen Cameron built this hotel. When he died they never stopped calling me Mrs. Cameron, even when I married you. It doesn't mean a thing."

"Swell. I'll see you at lunch."

Inez turned on her side, propping her head on her hand. The rough fabric of the bedspread had left a tracery of cross-hatchings on her breasts. "Kiss me, Chuck."

I bent over her. "Yes ma'am, Mrs. Cameron."

She turned her head away. "Oh, get out of here!"

I took off my ski socks, put on a pair of loafers and went downstairs. Inez Cameron Odlum, I thought. Proprietress of a million-buck hotel, complete with ski school, dogsleds, seven chefs, a staff of seventy, an indoor ice-skating rink, five acres of grounds here and another thirty at the ski slopes, a private beach on Whiteface Lake in summer—and a pet ski instructor for a husband. I felt abused for no reason at all. We argued about everything and about nothing. It was getting so we couldn't talk more than five minutes without stomping on each other's pride. It might have been her fault, but maybe it was mine. I went down to the bar for a drink.

The only customer was Mrs. Kemp. She stood there in the dim light, toying with an empty cocktail glass, a trim blonde with a good figure spelled out for you by her cashmere sweater and paisley lounging slacks.

"Another one of the same, Sammy," I told the barman. "It's on the house."

"Right. What's yours, Chuck?"

"Martini."

"Two martinis then. Coming up."

"No thank you. I'd really rather not," Mrs. Kemp said, smiling slightly at my reflection in the mirror behind the bar. "One cocktail before lunch is all I want, Mr.—Odlum, isn't it? The ski school?"

"That's right, Mrs. Kemp."

"Drumming up trade? I hate to disappoint you, but I never had a pair of skis on in my life. I wouldn't know how to begin."

She had a pleasant way of talking. It wasn't the words, it was how she said them, slightly husky-voiced and with an undertone of restrained delight, as if she wanted to get to know you better. I watched Sammy get the gin and vermouth from the back bar. I said, "Lots of people start skiing when they're twice your age." That was true enough, for she couldn't have been more than twenty-three or twenty-four. She had clear, fair skin and pale blue eyes. The only makeup she wore was a light shade of lipstick. Those pale blue eyes disturbed me and I didn't know why at first. I took a closer look and she stared back at me, her lips parting in another little smile. Then I knew what it was about those eyes. There are huskies that have eyes like that, pale blue and startlingly depthless.

Sammy brought my drink. I raised the cocktail glass to Mrs. Kemp and took a sip.

"He makes a good martini, doesn't he?" she said.

"The best, Mrs. Kemp." Sammy beamed at us and began to rearrange the bottles on the back bar. "But I didn't want to see you about skiing. The hotel owes you an apology, Mrs. Kemp."

Those depthless blue eyes stared at me and one of the arched blond eyebrows lifted. "Oh?"

"I understand you had a little trouble with one of the staff."

"It wasn't anything, really. I'd already forgotten about it."

"The manager wanted to sack him."

"Gosh, I'm sorry to hear that. You mean the dogsled driver, don't you?"

"Uh-huh."

"I wish there were something I could do."

"There is."

"I thought you said the manager fired him."

"I said he wanted to. I stopped him. I'm leaving it up to you, Mrs. Kemp."

"*You* are?"

"I own Whiteface Hotel or that is, my wife does."

"Mrs. Cameron? But I thought your name—"

"Odlum, that's right."

She let that ride. "It's funny how it happened, Mr. Odlum. I can't help thinking I'm partly responsible. But Jack's a nice boy and I wouldn't want you to fire him."

"Swell. You're a sport, Mrs. Kemp."

"You see, it was after the sled ride this morning. We got to talking. I never saw a husky before and I asked Jack some questions about them. Well, one thing led to another and he walked me up to my room. Then he said a funny thing. You know what he said? It was my eyes—my eyes were just like a husky's. I guess the idea amused me because I asked him in what way. He—well, he took a closer look. Then he—"

"Look, Mrs. Kemp. Don't feel you have to explain it."

"But I want to. It was all so innocent. His face got

very close and then he kissed me. Ever so gently, Mr. Odlum. Like a question. I could have handled it. I've had passes made at me before." The depthless eyes narrowed slightly with remembered anger. "But your Mr. Rowe came along. I'm sorry it happened, but I'm sorrier he popped up when he did. I'm a big girl, Mr. Odlum."

I liked her suddenly, probably because the anger in her eyes was for Kirby Rowe. I finished my drink and turned away from the bar. Then I said, "He was right, Mrs. Kemp."

"Who," she asked frostily, "Mr. Rowe?"

"No. Jack, I mean. About your eyes."

"I don't know whether I should take that as a compliment or not."

I shrugged. "They're your eyes."

She stared at me for a second, then we both grinned.

"I'm Bunny," she said.

"Chuck."

"I like the way you handled it much better than Mr. Rowe, Chuck."

"About that skiing lesson, it's on the house whenever you want."

"Why, thank you, Chuck."

"It's more fun than an apology."

"Maybe I'll take you up on it one of these days."

"Swell. See you."

"So long."

All during lunch with Inez I couldn't forget those eyes.

CHAPTER TWO

Kirby Rowe came into the ski school office after lunch. I was stapling tags on gloves and pole straps for the afternoon lessons, blue tag for beginner and yellow for intermediate, and I made him wait. He didn't like it. When the last guest went outside zipping up her parka, he said, "It looks like your protégé took off after all."

"Jack?"

"He's supposed to be outside with the dogs. He isn't and they aren't. You sure can pick them, Chuck."

"Yeah? Find me someone else who can handle the huskies this side of Fairbanks, Alaska."

"Well, we have a lot of guests waiting out there in the cold snow."

"You check the kennels?"

"I called his room, that's all."

"Okay, I'll take care of it."

I went outside. It was still snowing and a wind had whipped up off Whiteface Lake, blowing the snow into drifts. I waved at the skiers waiting in the bus and walked around behind the hotel to the dog run.

"Jack?" I called. "Hey, Jack, you around?"

The huskies were hunkered down in the snow in pairs behind the wire fence. They always paired off like that to keep warm, but their heads came up as I reached the fence and their fierce eyes watched me eagerly. They wanted to run. Nothing else satisfied them.

"Jack?"

No answer. I started to move away from the fence, but then he called me. "Just a second, be right with you."

Beyond the dog run we have five two-room cabins for the overflow crowd in summer. Now they were empty, except for the middle one where Jack had his room. He banged the door shut, buttoned up his mackinaw and ran down the cabin steps. A few minutes later he had all the dogs harnessed and the sleds ready to run.

"Didn't Rowe call you?" I asked him.

"On the phone? It didn't ring."

"Okay, shake a leg. They're waiting."

He got up behind the rear sled. "Mush, boys, mush!" he shouted, and the dogs began to run.

On a hunch I opened the wire fence and walked through the empty dog run to the cabin. The door started to open when I reached it. Bunny Kemp came out.

"Oh," she said. "Hello."

I just looked at her.

"There isn't anything I can say, is there? I—"

I was madder than I should have been. "Listen," I said, "you can give it away or sell it or display it in Macy's window, but don't do any of it with the staff on the staff's time."

Her depthless blue eyes narrowed and she slapped my face. Then I watched her walk through the dog run and out the gate and out of sight around the front of the hotel.

Driving out to the ski slopes I told myself she'd given me a sucker story and damn near got away with it. But so what? If Kirby Rowe found out, it would only vindicate my judgment of Jack McCall. With that kind of merchandise up for grabs, plenty of better men than Jack would have been guilty of a hallway kiss or a few minutes' delay harnessing the dogs. What difference did it make? For some reason I thought of Inez stretched out on our bed with the sun lamp burning her body brown, but when she took the little plastic cups off her eyes, they weren't Inez's eyes at all. They were the flat, pale blue eyes of a husky.

That was when I knew why I was so mad. I wanted her. If it was for sale, or for rent, or up for grabs, I wanted Bunny Kemp. And even if it wasn't, I wanted her.

"Look out!"

I yanked the big steering wheel hard to the right. The afternoon bus coming up from Albany and Lake Placid zoomed by, its exhaust roaring. I felt a sick excitement churning inside me, and I had to grip the wheel hard to keep my hands from shaking.

I put the blue and yellow ski classes through their paces that afternoon. Straight runs down the beginners' slope for the blue, with a snowplow at the bottom and no, baby, no—when you fall keep your knees together and go back and down to one side and don't wait till you're out of control; and stem turns for the yellow, weight on the downslope ski and bend into it and pivot from the hips—but keep your fanny centered lady or you'll take a header. Then I shut the gas engine that drives the rope tow and herded the blues and yellows back into the bus.

I showered and shaved and had dinner with Inez and Kirby Rowe, Afterwards I wandered around through the lobby and the bar and the lounge and the nightclub, signing up skiers for tomorrow's lessons. That was my job and all it took was a smile and some friendly chatter. But all the time I was looking for Bunny Kemp. I didn't find her. I almost called her room. Then I thought of Jack's cabin. No, there was a night sled ride on Elaine Skinner's social schedule.

"Hi."

"Hello, Elaine."

"Why the long face?"

"Four lessons and all this night life. I must be getting old."

"You? You're not a day over thirty?"

I was twenty-nine. We gabbed a while and I had a drink with Elaine, then she wandered off. Later, after most of the guests had called it a night, I went upstairs.

Inez was already in bed. I stripped down to my shorts and T-shirt and climbed in alongside of her. She leaned over and kissed me. Her breath came shallow and fast.

"Come on," she said. "Come on."

I took her rudely and savagely, without any foreplay. All the while I had this image of Bunny Kemp's eyes in my head.

When I got up in the morning it was really snowing. I padded barefoot to the window and saw how it had piled up during the night in high drifts driven by the gusty wind off the lake. Inez rolled over in bed and turned on the radio. In a few minutes we got a weather report. Ten inches of snow had fallen during the night in Plattsburg and the thermometer had plunged to minus three degrees. Up here in the mountains it would five or ten degrees colder than that, so right away I knew we were in for one of those days.

I dressed and went downstairs. It was seven-thirty, still half an hour before early breakfast, but a lot of guests were already milling around the lobby. They were restless. They acted like commuters waiting for a train that hadn't shown up and they got I-told-you-so looks on their faces when I had Elaine Skinner announce over the P.A. that skiing and sled rides were canceled for the day. She also said, though, that there'd be skating on the indoor ice and a program of games and square dancing in the afternoon. That made them feel a little better, but not much.

Kirby Rowe saw me after breakfast. "Six checkouts already this morning," he said glumly.

"The trains running?"

"Way behind schedule."

"How's the liquor supply? There's going to be plenty of drinking today."

Inez came up behind me. "Don't project, darling," she said too sweetly. Kirby Rowe smiled at her.

"I got the long-range forecast on the phone," she told us. "They haven't seen anything like it since the fifty-inch fall in 1952. There's a low-pressure area sitting right over the mountains and they don't know when the snow will stop."

"In '52 we were sensible," Kirby Rowe said. "We closed up for the winter."

"Well, this winter's just an experiment," Inez reminded him.

It *was* an experiment. I'd talked Inez into keeping the hotel open the year round, and Kirby Rowe hadn't liked the idea. Previous winters he'd gone down to Miami Beach to manage a small hotel, coming back up here when the Whiteface opened for the Decoration Day weekend. But skiing had become a big thing in New York State, and I'd talked Inez into trying it out this winter. Every chance he got, Kirby Rowe downgraded the idea. In a way it had been a selfish idea with me, for I've skied all my life, and I thought I could really earn my keep at Whiteface in winter. That was another one of the things between me and Kirby Rowe, and it had rankled me all along. You could see that Inez would have preferred lolling in the southern sun till the end of May. I'd talked her into it, though, because the first winter of our marriage last year had made me feel like a kept man.

I walked away from them and then drifted back because Bunny Kemp was coming over to the desk. I got between her and Kirby Rowe so she'd have to talk to me. Probably she hadn't heard the announcement about skiing, because she was wearing a pair of stretch ski pants and a turtleneck sweater. The stretch pants were molded to her thighs and hips as snug as leotards. She had beautiful legs.

"Good morning, Mr. Odlum," she said, then patted her thighs. "You see, I decided to take you up on those skiing lessons. I bought these in town yesterday."

"I'm sorry, Mrs. Kemp, but there won't be any skiing today."

"Gosh, that's too bad. Are the roads passable?"

The abrupt switch surprised me. "Well, they usually run the snowplows through several times a day even before it stops snowing. They're liable to drift right over again in this wind. I'd say, rugged but passable."

"The reason I asked, my husband's driving up today."

That hit me below the belt, where my endocrines had done my thinking for me yesterday. All I could do was mumble something about hoping he'd have a good, safe drive.

Kirby Rowe cleared his throat and said, "Will you be changing to a double room, Mrs. Kemp?"

"Oh, I guess I should have told you sooner. I'm afraid I'll be checking out when Mr. Kemp gets here." She turned to me. "That's why I wanted those lessons this morning, Mr. Odlum. Well, next year maybe."

"Sure, maybe next year." I wandered off and across the lobby to the bar. Sammy was dusting off the jukebox, but when he saw me he came around behind the hardwood. "Isn't it a little early for you, Chuck?"

"Well, just make it a dry vermouth."

He poured and I drank. I had two more sitting there. I tried to tell myself Kemp's arrival was the best thing that could have happened to me. Cheating on your wife was one thing, but messing around with another man's wife was something else again. Not that I'd ever cheated on Inez; until Bunny Kemp came along I'd never had the itch. Sure, we weren't exactly happily married. I couldn't get over the idea that Inez was my wife at night in bed and Kirby Rowe's wife the rest of the time. But hell, that hardly made sense, for she could have married Kirby but had married me instead.

I'd put in three summers at Whiteface as a lifeguard. The first summer, a heart attack had killed Owen Cameron. Inez weathered it pretty well, and the next summer the staff thought she and Kirby Rowe were having an affair. It went on like that. If it ended, no one knew when—or why. But the summer before last, Inez got back from her Florida vacation about a month before Kirby returned from his Florida job. We started going around together. Until then I'd been spending most of my spare time, some of it in bed, with Elaine Skinner. When Kirby got back, Inez and I didn't stop. Two Thanksgivings ago, we got married. At first the staff would have put two bucks down to get your one that Kirby would quit. But he hadn't. Then one night Inez told me she was going to give him a raise. I'd told her it was her money.

"You don't think he deserves it?"

I shrugged.

"Well, let me tell you something. He asked me to marry him."

"Then why didn't you?"

We were in bed. Inez rubbed her body against mine

and purred. "Because this time I wanted a *man*. Oh, Kirby's all right but … how can I put it? Kirby's an indoor man. Pressed suits and neat ties and well-combed hair. I know that kind. I was married to one for five years. They can be very nice and very attentive, but effete. This time I wanted a man with lots of outdoor inclinations …"

"And muscles between his ears."

"… and only one indoor inclination."

"Like so?"

"Like … ah, Chuck …"

And afterwards, the steel-trap mind working again, she said, "His ego's been pretty badly bruised, you know."

"Huh? Who? Who's ego?"

"Kirby's. That's why I want to give him a raise. To three hundred a week, all right?"

"I said it's your money."

"Baby, baby, I don't want you to feel that way."

"You do whatever you think's right, Inez."

"Three hundred a week all year round, darling. And we can buy that big old mountain you were talking about and have our winter season and you can have your ski school. How's that?"

It was fine, of course. I'd wanted that ski school. But somehow that night I didn't think of it as a gift, or of Inez making the pet husband happy and the almost-husband happy with the same gesture. Maybe, though, that's behind the trouble between me and Inez. The way she worked it, almost from the start, she could have both her men. I'm not the jealous type. I never have been. But I was never married to a million bucks, till Inez. And I couldn't get over the notion that I bored her—except at night. Drinking, it came out something like this: Kirby would bore her at night and I'd bore her during the day. She had Kirby for the business of the day and me for the pleasure of the night. Two half men equal one whole man.

"You," I told Sammy in the bar the day Bunny Kemp's husband was arriving, "are looking at a trained seal."

"You," Sammy said, "are drinking too much."

After the first two vermouths I'd switched to bourbon on the rocks. "Mrs. Cameron'll raise the roof if she sees you like this in the morning."

"Yaaa," I said.

"Yeah."

Then Elaine Skinner's face swam in the back bar mirror next to mine. "You better see Wally," she said. Wally was the bandleader. "He isn't exactly kicking his heels together over the prospect of an afternoon square dance." Elaine made a face. "Say, did you hear a rumor Prohibition's coming back or something?"

"Man was thirsty," Sammy said.

"Why, you'll drink up all your wife's profits."

"You, too?" I said.

"I—I'm sorry. That was clumsy of me." Elaine bit her lip "And that was even clumsier. You run along and see Wally."

I ran along and saw Wally. I gave him the old get-in-there-and-fight routine. He didn't like it, but I sold it to him. It was one of those days. I helped Elaine organize a game of charades in the lounge. I scrounged around in the cellar storeroom with a couple of the bellboys until we found two cartons of straw hats left over from New Year's Eve. They'd help set the tone for the square dance. I did my best to placate some guests who couldn't ice skate because we'd run out of skates. By the time lunch rolled around my head felt like the sound box of Wally Shevlin's bass fiddle with Wally plucking the strings.

Orin Kemp arrived at three-thirty. I was holding down the desk so the desk clerk could grab a quick, late lunch. Kemp was a big red-faced man in a trench coat and a snap-brim hat. He wore glasses, and the warm air in the lobby had steamed them. He removed them and polished the lenses with his scarf. He had dark, deep-set eyes which wore that look of vague anger you associate with unsuccessful or frustrated men. I figured him for about forty.

"Phew!" he said. "What a drive. Place in here I can get a drink?"

"The bar." I pointed.

"I'm Kemp. Orin Kemp. The wife—"

"Oh, are you planning on staying with us, Mr. Kemp? We could give you a double."

I said that because I'd noticed his suitcase. It was a bulging gladstone with thick leather straps. He set it down on the floor near his feet.

"No, we'll be, taking off as soon as the missus can pack. You tell her I'm here, huh? I'll be in the bar when she's ready."

"Right, Mr. Kemp."

He lifted the gladstone and headed for the bar. The weight of the suitcase made his right shoulder sag. Through the doorway of the bar I could see him put the bag down at his feet and lean his elbows on the hardwood.

I told the phone girl in the little PBX room behind the desk I'd be gone a few minutes. Earlier, I had seen Bunny Kemp, in flannel shirt and jeans, going into the nightclub for the square dance. We had pushed the tables back against the walls and there was plenty of room for dancing.

Wally Shevlin was calling the dance and playing a

squeaky hillbilly number on his fiddle. Sweat streamed down his face under the straw hat he wore. He gave me a weak, set-upon grin and stamped his cowboy boots and stroked his fiddle and chanted.

"Promenade and ..."

I looked for Bunny Kemp's blond hair, but all the girls were wearing straw hats as they came promenading by on the arms of their partners.

"Swing your partner, skip to the ..."

The couples whirled, arms linked. Then I saw them—Jack McCall and Bunny. She was smiling and looking up at his face when they swung around. Her startling eyes gleamed and her cheeks were flushed with excitement. Jack's eyes never left her face.

"Mrs. Kemp," I called.

She squeezed Jack's arm and came over to me, unconsciously keeping time to the fiddle. She was panting and fine beads of sweat covered her upper lip. "I haven't done that in years," she said. "It was fun."

"Your husband's here," I said coldly.

With other people you could tell by the eyes, but you couldn't read anything in Bunny Kemp's depthless eyes. They were beautiful, but like glass. They never changed at all. They were so strange, so completely flat, you almost wondered if she saw out of them like other people did. But her face changed. The smile faded, the cheeks drew in, the full-lipped mouth became smaller. "Oh. Yes, of course. I'm glad he made it all right."

"He's waiting in the bar, Mrs. Kemp."

"I'll pack."

She went out to the lobby. In a little while Jack came over. "What's with her?" he wanted to know.

"Mr. Kemp just got in. They'll be checking out."

Jack's eyes widened. He took off his straw hat and handed it to me without a word and started to walk away.

"It's 305," I said.

Jack turned and glared at me, then kept going. I left the straw hat on a table and went back to the desk.

Behind it there was a wooden partition. On the far side we kept the hotel records and did the billing. From the lobby you couldn't see anyone sitting there. I smoked a cigarette and went back of the partition to figure out Bunny Kemp's bill. I was almost finished when I heard their voices.

"You little fool," I heard Kemp say. "Who was the guy?"

"What's the difference?" Bunny said. "What difference does it make?"

"I said, who was the guy?"

"Just a man who works at the hotel."

"What he want?"

"Nothing. We got a little friendly."

"A little friendly! Are you nuts?"

"We danced together this afternoon, that's all."

"All? I got to sweat it out while you have yourself a ball."

"You have patience. I get all itchy waiting. I would have gone crazy, just waiting. You don't have to make a federal case out of it."

"Don't even say that, you little bitch!"

"Orin, I only—"

"Shut up. Are you nuts or something?"

"Stop raising your voice." There was a pause. Then Bunny said, "Is that it?"

"Yeah, sure."

"You should have left it in the car."

"The car? Are you nuts?"

"Why don't you wear it around your neck like a sandwich sign? Here we have …"

"Shut up, you crazy little bitch!"

"Orin, I'm warning you."

I don't know why, but I didn't want them to see me pop up from behind the partition. I went out through the PBX room and came up behind them. "Here's your bill, Mrs. Kemp," said. "Hope you enjoyed yourself here."

Orin Kemp whirled. His angry eyes had narrowed to slits. His big hands balled into fists as I handed the bill in his direction. He took it, glanced at it without seeing the figures and peeled some money off the roll in his pocket. He had the bill in one hand and the money in the other. I lifted the gladstone by its handle and said, "I'll have a boy put this in your car." The bag was astonishingly heavy. It must have weighed over a hundred pounds.

"Here, I'll take that!" Orin Kemp shouted. He shoved the bill and the money at Bunny. I put the bag down and he hefted it. Bunny paid the bill. A few minutes later they left. I went to the door and watched them get into their car. It was a gray sedan, what you could see of it under the snow, three or four years old. The rear tires had chains on them.

I watched them drive off into the snow.

CHAPTER THREE

"Where are they? Is that them driving away?"

I turned away from the door and almost bumped heads with Jack McCall. "You mean the Kemps?"

"Who the hell else do you think I meant?"

"Keep your shirt on, Jack. It was the Kemps all

right."

"Where they going?"

"How should I know? Back to New York probably. That's where they came from."

"She didn't want to go with him," Jack said bleakly. "She didn't want to."

"Of course not," I said. I had a mean hangover from the morning drinking. "She wanted to stay here so you could stare into those husky eyes."

"Give me the station wagon keys," Jack said suddenly. "I'm going after them."

"You're out of your mind."

"She—she wants me to. I could tell. She's afraid of him. Give me those keys."

"I can't. I've got to drive some people down to the station at Lake Placid."

"Use the bus."

"And I wouldn't anyway," I added, ignoring his suggestion. "Leave it alone, Jack. They're married. You know, husband and wife?" It made me feel a little better saying it like that.

"Give me those keys or I'll take them off of you!" Jack shouted. We stood very close. Angry blood rose up and darkened the skin of his face. I was facing in toward the lobby and I could see a few people watching us.

"Give them to me!" he yelled again, his face about three inches from mine.

I raised my hands and put the palms flat against his chest and shoved. He stumbled back a step. Off balance like that, he swung at me. His fist sailed past my ear and his arm wrapped around my neck. Over his shoulder I saw Inez coming toward us across the lobby, walking fast. He leaned on me for a second, bending forward, leaving his middle open. I wanted to end it fast and I didn't want it to look like a fight. I balled my right fist and let him have it short and hard, without any body swing behind it, at the belt line. He sagged against me and held on. I tried to push him away. He clung to me, getting his breath. He grappled me back toward the desk. His anger was for Orin Kemp, but I was handy.

"Chuck, what's the matter with you?" Inez said in a furious whisper. I looked at her. Jack let go, moved back a step and hit me. It didn't feel like much, but my jaw went numb and I felt my knees going rubbery. Then I was sitting down with my back against the desk, licking blood off my lips.

I got up fast, but Inez stood between us with her back to me. "You're finished here, McCall," I heard her say. "I want you out of here by morning."

"That suits me. But I want transportation for the dogs."

"We'll buy the dogs from you. And stop shouting."

"They're not for sale."

Inez looked at me. "You handle it, Chuck. Without using your fists, damn you," she said in that same furious whisper. "Then I want to see you—in our room." She invited the circle of hotel guests into the bar for drinks on the house, and they broke up to follow her.

"What the hell, Jack," I said, "I'm sorry I tried to push you around."

"Yeah? You hypocritical bastard, giving me that blue-nosed lecture. I saw the way you were looking at Bunny. You wanted some of that, too, didn't you?"

If we kept it up, we'd start swinging again. I said, "Arrange any kind of transportation you need for the dogs. We'll pay for it—with your two weeks' severance pay."

Before he could answer, I walked away. I couldn't

hang around the lobby because they'd start drifting back from the bar and asking me about the fight. I headed for the nightclub, but the square dance was breaking up. I shrugged and went upstairs to our room.

Waiting, I smoked three or four cigarettes and belted a bottle of bourbon we kept in the night table. Inez made me wait an hour. It wasn't till she came in that I began to feel like a naughty kid being punished by his mother.

Inez shut the door, looked at me and the uncapped bottle, set her arms akimbo and shook her head.

I said, "If I promise to be a good boy the rest of the day can I have supper and watch TV?"

"It's nothing to joke about, Chuck. We can't have that kind of behavior in the hotel. Maybe now you realize why Kirby Rowe's still an indispensable man around here."

"Sure. Jack would have mopped up the floor with him."

"That's beside the point. Anyhow, you weren't doing too well when I broke it up. You were drunk this morning, Chuck. In the morning. You were fighting like a roughneck this afternoon. What are you going to do tonight, attack or seduce one of the guests?"

"Come here and I'll show you," I said. She didn't move. I went over to her. She'd never minded making love after one of our arguments. Sometimes I thought she even liked it.

"Keep your hands off me. I know you're virile. What will that prove?"

I put my arms around her. She got her hands free and hit me with both of them, one very fast after the other, in the mouth. "I don't want a roughneck around this hotel," she said. "And I won't have a roughneck for a husband."

"There's always Kirby," I said.

First I thought she was going to hit me again, but she only bit her lip and looked at me. I went over to the bed and sat on the edge, putting my face in my hands. The bourbon was going around and around in my head.

"I didn't mean that," I said. "I'm all mixed up."

"Then what did you mean?"

"I'm all mixed up. I'm sorry, Inez."

I didn't hear her come over. Her hand touched my head, then she ran her fingers through my hair. I looked up and she probed my lips gently. "Try to behave yourself. And I'm sorry if I hurt you."

"Yeah, sure."

"Try to be a good boy."

I shut my eyes. I could sense her lingering presence. I could smell her perfume. Then after a while she went away, and the door opened and closed.

Try to be a good boy. *Damn*.

Well maybe, I thought. I don't know. I always managed to act like a kid around Inez. But hell, I can handle myself.

I've knocked around most of twenty-nine years, taking each year as it came.

Try to be a good boy! Damn it all to hell! She had the hotel. She had the money. And when she wanted what she considered a mature man she had Kirby Rowe. I wanted out all of a sudden. I'd never wanted out so bad in my life. Just sitting there, thinking, knowing I'd acted like a fool with Inez, made it feel like the walls were closing in on me.

The wind moaned outside. I picked up the bourbon bottle and drank. I wondered if Orin Kemp and his wife had reached Lake Placid yet. I wondered what those eyes were looking at right now.

CHAPTER FOUR

The next morning, which was a Friday, I didn't even stay at the hotel long enough to eat breakfast. I had to get off by myself and think things out. If I hung around I would have blown up. I could feel it. Anyhow, I rationalized, there was plenty to do down at the ski slope.

Some time during the night it had stopped snowing, but driving down toward the slope in the Whiteface's four-wheel-drive Willys I caught a weather report which said we could expect more of the same by nightfall.

It was a cold but clear morning with very little wind. Across the frozen and snow-covered lake you could see the bare crag of Whiteface Mountain and, backdropping it, the sky was that incredible blue you see only in winter, when the ground and the trees are white mantled like a Kodachrome Christmas card. I had loaded my skis and poles in the station wagon. As I turned off the main highway to Lake Placid and started climbing the secondary road up into the hills, I began to feel pretty good. The state snow plows had already come through, and the road was sanded on the bad turns. Pine boughs hung heavily under their loads of snow. The sun was so dazzling on the snow that I had to put on my ski goggles.

After a big storm there's plenty you have to do to get a ski slope in shape. Usually I called up a couple of high school kids in Lake Placid who had practically been weaned on skis to help me, but this time I didn't want company. Just knowing I'd have the whole day to myself for the kind of work I could do, well, I felt the tension dropping away.

I parked the station wagon in front of the lodge we'd built at the base of the slope last fall and got out to case the situation. I whistled. The main slope had drifted over and the trails, out of sight behind thick stands of pine, would be worse. There are two basic things you have to do. We didn't have any of the big snow-cats the state uses on its slopes, so that meant I'd have to sidestep down the hill on skis, packing the powder down on its old snow base. Then, using a shovel and my skis, I'd have to firm a trail for the rope tow. The job would take three men, working hard, all morning. I wondered if I could finish it alone by nightfall.

I clomped into the lodge with my skis. Stacking them against the wall, I built a big fire in the fieldstone fireplace. Pretty soon the flames were roaring up the flue like far-off thunder, their glow reflected on the bare split logs of the lodge. I put up some coffee on the grill behind the long counter and waxed my skis while waiting for it to boil. On the soft, fresh snow I'd need plenty of wax. I used up a book of matches melting it against the plastic running surfaces of the skis so it would last out the day. By the time I finished, the coffee was boiling and its aroma filled the lodge. I put five strips of bacon on the grill and watched them sizzle and quiver, then I fried three eggs in their fat and made myself some toast. For no reason at all I smiled. I felt good. Yesterday seemed a year ago in another country.

Eating breakfast, I sat facing the big picture window at the back of the lodge. Through it you could see the wide, white swooping expanse of the main slope, the rope tow pulleys with the cable hanging slack and the snow-mantled stand of pine that hid the advanced skiing trail. There wasn't a sound except for the fire. I had the world all to myself.

When I finished eating I went into the supply room and poked around awhile, straightening out the skis we keep at the lodge for last-minute rentals. We had posters on the wall showing the ski trails and skiers at Garmisch, St. Anton and Klosters. They didn't have a thing on me, I thought. I had my mountain.

I went outside with my skis and clamped the bindings. Then I started up the main slope. Using my poles I could go straight up without herringboning because the snow was so soft. Standing at the top you could see Lake Placid and Mirror Lake and Whiteface Lake. Nestled in its valley between Lake Placid and Mirror Lake, the town of Lake Placid was rows of toy houses flanking a make-believe road on which tiny dots that were toy cars were moving. And you could see the fangs of half the Adirondacks range biting up at the blue sky. To hell with Kirby Rowe, I thought. To hell with Jack McCall and Bunny Kemp, and to hell with Inez, if that was the way she wanted it. This was living.

The next couple of hours I sidestepped down the hill four times. That gave us twenty-five feet of good skiing snow. I climbed back up the hill and stood poised at the top for a moment. The air was crisp and clear and I was sweating despite the cold. I pushed off with my poles and swooped down the hill picking up speed. There is no way a man can move faster without mechanical help than on skis. I went down hard and fast, not turning, following the fall line. I wanted speed. I wanted to feel the rushing wind whipping at my face. Then at the bottom I bent and pivoted into a Christie stop, the suddenly turned edges of my skis gouging snow that came back down in a fine icy spray.

"Hello there!"

I should have recognized her voice right away, but I was away in my own private world and it took some coming back. She stood behind the station wagon, waving. Another car was parked there. I hadn't heard it drive up. A gray sedan with a foot of snow on its roof. The Kemps' car.

I poled over to her without talking.

"I thought I might find you here this morning, Chuck," she said. "Boy, you really know how to handle yourself on those skis. I was watching you."

"I thought you'd be in New York by now," I said.

Then I saw the fender of their car. It was crumpled and bent. It looked as if a mechanic had straightened it out enough so the wheel could turn.

She shook her head. "Are you mad at me?"

"I don't know you well enough to be mad at you, Bunny."

"Care for a smoke?"

I nodded. "Come on inside. There's coffee."

I took off my skis and left them on the rack in front of the lodge. Inside, I put two more big logs on the fire, then placed the coffee pot back on the grill.

"You have breakfast?"

"Uh-huh. Just coffee will be fine."

We sat and smoked without talking for a while. She wore those stretch ski pants that fitted her, as stretch pants should, like skin. When she got up to get the coffee, her buttocks looked as firm as marble. I watched their neat small pelvic swing and had to look away in a hurry when she turned around with the coffee pot.

"I don't get it," I said. "What happened? Where's your husband?"

"Poor Orin," she said, but her face was all set to break into a smile. "We didn't get three miles down the road yesterday when we went into a skid. You saw the car."

"Anybody hurt?"

"Orin. He sprained his ankle pretty badly. We're staying at a motel down the road until he feels well enough to drive."

"What about you?"

"I said I was too scared to drive on ice after the accident. There's lots of ice on the roads where the plows have come through."

"You drove up here."

She set her cup down. "More coffee?"

I filled the cup for her. When I put the coffee pot down, our hands touched. Her fingers closed for a second over mine. Just touching her hand I felt a little icy tingle race down my spine.

She took her hand away to light another cigarette. "I told you I might take you up on those skiing lessons. Well, here I am."

Just then the telephone rang. It wasn't a phone open to the public lines, you could only reach the hotel with it. I let it ring five or six times.

"Aren't you going to answer it?"

I went over to the counter and picked up the receiver. "Odlum," I said into it.

"Kirby Rowe, Chuck. We have a bunch of people pestering us about skiing."

"It's still all snowed in, Kirby," I said. "I'm working on it. Tell them to try Fawn Ridge."

"How about this afternoon?"

"Tell them tomorrow morning, if we're lucky."

"Oh, that's too bad. Need any help?"

"Got all the help I can use."

"Right. Let me know if there's any change."

"Okay." I hung up. "Well, all set?" I asked Bunny.

"Private lessons. I heard that. I think I like it."

"Come on. What size shoe do you take?"

"Seven."

I got her a pair of six-foot skis and a pair of size seven boots out of the supply room. She kicked off her galoshes and shoes and sat down on a bench so I could lace the ski boots for her.

"Hold it a minute," I said. I waxed the running surfaces of her skis while she watched me with cool interest. At least it looked cool. You could never tell with those eyes.

"Easiest place to put them on is right here," I said. "You stand up alongside the bench and put one foot up."

"These boots weigh a ton."

"You'll get used to them."

I set the skis parallel on the bench and she put her right foot up. She bent over me while I clamped the binding. Her blond hair brushed my face.

"Other one," I said.

She put her other foot up. The seam of her ski pants ran straight without a wrinkle to her crotch. I was all thumbs clamping the other binding.

"These are safety bindings," I said, needing to talk. "If you take a bad spill they'll break away before you break a bone."

"It's nice to know."

I brought her the poles. I showed her how to sling the straps over her wrists and grab the leather and the haft together. Then she clattered on her skis across the wood floor, I opened the door and we were outside. She waited while I clamped my own bindings.

"Tow's not working. Man forgot to shovel it," I said. "So your first lesson is learning how to climb up hill."

"Uh-oh. That sounds like work."

"It's a snap. Let's go."

I gave her an hour and a half of steady coaching. She picked up the fundamentals very quickly. She had a natural athlete's fluid, effortless grace and she seemed to be enjoying herself. We'd go up about fifty yards, first sidestepping, later herringboning, and I taught her how to turn by lifting the tails of her skis and rotating them one at a time, and how to keep from slipping down the fall line by edging in. Then I'd have her make some straight runs down the fall line. The first time she took a header and her left ski binding broke away. Her face was covered with snow, but she got up smiling. I took off my mittens and brushed her off. Her skin was cool and smooth and her cheeks were rosy from the climbing.

"I like it when you touch me," she said.

I just looked at her.

"I—I'm sorry. I shouldn't have said that."

"Come on."

By the third downhill run she was able to execute a pretty fair snowplow. She looked at me very earnestly when I gave her instructions, and she followed them to a "T." She was a very good pupil and I liked teaching her. It made me feel good. But it made me think of Inez, too; I couldn't teach Inez anything. With Inez, somehow I always wound up being just a kid. The beach boy. The ski school instructor. With Bunny it couldn't have been more different. I had an expert's calm confidence with Bunny, and I had a notion that feeling wouldn't stop with skiing.

Toward the end of the hour and a half I gave her the fundamentals of the snow plow turn. She followed everything I said and everything I did with a frown of concentration on her face. "Remember," I said, summing up after I'd shown her how to do it. "Bend into it, weight on downhill ski, turn the downhill toe in and swing from the knees and hips but don't lean over sideways."

She tried it, and laughed with delight when she found she could do it. Pretty soon I had her traversing down the hill from the level spot three-quarters of the way up, cutting back and forth across the fall line.

"You're really some teacher, Chuck," she said a little breathlessly at the bottom. "You could teach an elephant how to ski."

"You're no elephant. I could have you doing the slalom inside of two weeks."

"Thank you, kind sir, for the compliment."

"Tired?"

"No, but let's stop. I'm hungry as an elephant."

"You work up an appetite skiing."

"Do we have to go back?"

"No reason why. There's plenty to eat in the lodge."

We took off our skis and stacked them. Then I turned, heading for the lodge. Something hit my back. It was a snow ball. Bunny packed another one, laughing, and threw it. I ducked and it whizzed over my head. I scooped up some snow and flung it at Bunny. She went on laughing and we went on throwing, chasing each other around and around the lodge tossing snow balls like a couple of kids. If I tried that once with Inez, I couldn't help thinking, she'd have just looked at me and that would have ended it.

Then I ducked around a corner of the building and waited. I heard Bunny coming. I scooped up snow in both hands and stood up just as she turned the corner. She ran into my arms, unable to stop. I rubbed the snow on the back of her windbreaker. I felt her arms tighten on my ribs and her hands squeezed the small of my back. We looked into each other's face, laughing.

I don't know who stopped laughing first, but Bunny broke away from me and we looked at each other soberly for a minute, then smiled again and ran into the lodge.

I replenished the wood on the fire and in a little while had a good blaze going. Bunny took off her windbreaker and peeled two sweaters off over her head. "This is a lovely place," she said. "Bearskin rug and all. I love it."

She sat down and removed her boots while I took six hamburger patties from the refrigerator and plunked them on the grill. When they started to sizzle I said, "Ketchup and mustard under the counter."

"You do the work. I'm just relaxing. Gee, I feel good. I tingle all over." She looked good, too, healthy and windblown, her blond hair in a kind of artful disarray, her cheeks red, her lips parted slightly. I knocked over the ketchup bottle looking at her. She smiled. "You'll make me blush," she said.

I split the hamburger rolls and toasted them a little on the grill. I had already put up a fresh pot of coffee. "Black all right?" I asked when it had begun to boil.

"That's the way I like it."

"Rum?"

"You mean you actually have rum here? I *love* this place. I just love it."

"It's not for the paying customers," I said.

"You know, I think I'm going to become a real ski enthusiast—what do you call them?"

"Snow bunnies," I said. We both laughed. "Say, what is Bunny short for anyhow?"

"Bonita. But nobody calls me that."

I spiked our coffee with thick, dark Jamaica rum. We ate without talking, ravenously. We had three cups of coffee and the third was half-and-half. I put more wood on the fire and sat down in front of it on the bearskin rug. Bunny came over and sat down alongside of me, watching the fire dance and leap.

After a while I said, "How do your insteps feel?"

"My insteps?"

"If you're going to be sore from your first day's skiing, that's where it usually gets you."

"Oh, I see what you mean. Leaning forward with all your weight from the ankles all the time." She drew her knees up and touched her insteps through the white athletic socks she wore. "Well, what do you know," she said. "Kind of tender at that."

"I'll rub them for you."

Obediently she slipped the elastic bands at the ankles of her ski pants and took off her socks. She put her bare feet up on my lap and I began to massage the insteps.

"Next time wear two pairs of socks," I advised her.

"I'll remember that."

"Feel better?"

"Yes. You've got magic fingers. That feels wonderful."

I massaged the firm flesh of her insteps, feeling the delicate bones and cartilage under it. Her skin was very white. I looked at her face. She had her hands stiffly at her sides, palms down on the bearskin rug, leaning her weight on them. Her head was thrown back and the cords stood out on her neck. Her eyes looked like blue glass. The firelight flickered in them.

I ran one hand lightly up the outside of her ski pants to her knee. She didn't move. Her lips parted. She had even little teeth, as white as the snow outside. I let my hand go up higher and she made a soft eager wordless sound.

"Bunny," I said.

"Snow bunny," she said, but her voice broke on the

last syllable.

I leaned my weight on her and she stretched out her legs and we lay facing each other on the bearskin rug. One of her legs moved and came between my legs.

"Bunny?" I said in a hoarse whisper.

"Yes, yes...."

I kissed her. I stiffened, thinking of her coming out of Jack McCall's cabin, but her lips parted under mine and the thought went away. Then I was fumbling with the zipper at the side of her ski pants. She helped me with it, laughing a little at my eager clumsiness, then kissing me again and letting me peel the tight black stretch pants down her legs. She was unbuttoning her flannel shirt when I finished. Her legs were smooth and firm like ivory, as were her shoulders. I kissed the base of her throat and felt a pulse beating there. Then she slipped out of her bra and panties smoothly, without haste, while I fumbled with my own clothing.

We came together very quickly. We were both ready for it, the rhythm sweeping us up as if we'd known the secrets of each other's body a thousand times but each time fresh and exciting like the first. The rhythm mounted and we reached our climaxes together and for a long moment time and the world and everything went up the flue with the roaring flames and it was the best moment a man and a woman can have, the high fine exquisite moment of passion completely and frankly shared.

Maybe if, at that moment, someone could have told us all the rest was downhill hard and fast on a long desperate slide, it wouldn't have mattered. But of course there was no one to tell us.

CHAPTER FIVE

We sat on the bearskin rug, smoking cigarettes and watching the fire die. Bunny wore her bra and panties and sat with her knees drawn up, her hands locked around them and her head on my shoulder. We'd hardly said a word since making love. It was the third cigarette for each of us. We didn't look at each other. There was a lot I wanted to say, but the words wouldn't come.

In a way, with our ski clothes strewn around and the thick soft woolly feel of the bearskin and what was left of the glowing logs settling on the andirons, it was like a scene from an erotic dream. I didn't want it to end like that. I wanted it to be real, but I could find no words.

"It's getting cold," Bunny said after a long time.

"Want me to put on more wood?"

She shook her head. "I better get dressed."

As she started to rise, I touched her leg. "Listen," I said.

"I don't want to talk, Chuck."

"Sorry?"

"No—oh, no."

She kneeled there and reached for her flannel shirt, the dying firelight glowing on the outthrust curve of her hip. I flipped my cigarette into the fire and watched her movements. There was a word for what we had done. It didn't matter how I felt or how I hoped she felt. She had a husband. I had a wife. It didn't matter what had driven us to it. The word was, and is, adultery.

"Listen," I said. "I—"

She shrugged her shoulders into the plaid flannel shirt but didn't button it. "I like you, snow bunny," I said.

She smiled at me, just with one side of her mouth. Maybe she felt remorse, maybe the lopsided smile, the part of her that wouldn't smile, was for remorse. All of a sudden I had to know about Jack McCall. She'd come out of his cabin a few minutes after he had. Here, with me, surfeit, she'd sat silently a long time. Her husband and what she was going to do didn't mean a thing right now—I had to find out about Jack.

"Listen," I said, "when you—"

It was as if she could read my mind. Her smile was radiant then. "Silly," she said. "I didn't go to bed with Jack McCall. What kind of girl do you think I am?" She asked that not angrily, but teasingly.

She buttoned the shirt. I said, "Don't mind me. I'm sorry. Another thing." I felt a lump in my throat. I swallowed.

"What is it, Chuck?"

"This wasn't just a roll in the hay. I wanted you to know that."

"Of course, it wasn't. You didn't have to tell me. I knew it. Chuck—me, too."

I watched the fire awhile. Then I said, "You going back to him?"

"Orin? He's my husband."

"Do you love him?"

She didn't answer that.

"I love you, Bunny. I love you."

"You hardly even know me. You don't know anything about me."

"I know all I have to know," I said stubbornly. "I know that I love you."

She dropped her ski pants and came down on me. I held her. I could feel her heart pounding. "I love you, too, Chuck. I do, I do."

"Bunny?"

"I love you."

"No listen. We can get away together. I don't know where, but if we want to we can. Bunny?"

"I'm listening. I love the sound of the music." I couldn't see her face. I stroked her hair. The way her voice sounded I thought she was crying, or at least trying not to cry.

"We can work it out together," I said. "We—"

The door creaked and the late afternoon wind which had whipped up slammed it back against the split logs of the wall. Bunny scampered away from me and I looked up. Jack McCall came in talking. He didn't see us down there in front of the fire right away.

"They said I might find you here, Chuck," he said. "They're giving me a hard time with the dogs. What you said about severance pay is okay with me, but they...." His voice trailed off. He had come in with his eyes on the open door of the supply room. He thought I was in there. That doorway was on the same wall as the fireplace, and he almost walked right past us before he saw us. Bunny was crouching with the tails of her flannel shirt down around her legs. I started to get up. Jack said, "So that's why you called the whole thing off."

At first I thought he was talking to me and it didn't make sense. Then I realized he was talking to Bunny. He smirked as she got to her feet. "You're nothing but a little—"

She slapped his face. "Don't talk to me like that," she said. "Get out of here."

He caught her wrist, twisting it, and shoved her

back against the wall. I saw red. I jumped him, clubbing the side of his neck with my fist. He stumbled sideways two steps and I charged at him blindly. He got out of the way and pushed me as I went past him. I caught the supply room door frame and swung around. He was ready for me, his fists up. This time I came to him slowly, shooting out a left jab which he picked off in air.

"I got no fight with you, Chuck," he said, panting.

I tried the jab again. It split his lips. He hooked his own left at my ear, and it rang with the blow. Wary and cool, he waited for me to move. All I wanted to do was hurt him. I ducked my head and charged. That was a mistake. I wound up on the floor, looking up at him. He backed away so I could get to my feet. I saw Bunny edging sideways toward the counter. Very fast on his feet, Jack circled me. I drew blood from his mouth again. He countered automatically with his right. I ducked under it, planting my left hard under his ribs. He held on and I butted him. I heard his teeth click. Then he brought his knee up and that would have put me out of the fight except that I turned my thigh and took it on the outside of my leg. He stepped back and I hit him going away. He sailed through the doorway of the supply room. I followed him on the run. He tripped on one of the small three-legged stools in there that we use for fitting boots. When he got up I was wild with a right. He came in very close and stomped on my bare foot. I bent over and he rabbit-punched me. I held on to keep from falling and hit him where they would have taken the round away.

All that time it took him to get as mad as I was. He doubled over and staggered back against the wall where the ski poles were stacked. He grabbed one of them and charged me. I heard Bunny cry out. Until then I hadn't realized that she was in the supply room with us. Jack swung the aluminum ski pole. The basket and the wicked curved point whistled over my head. When he swung it again I grabbed the basket and held on. I grabbed the haft too, above his hand, and still holding the leather thongs of the basket, pushed him back with the pole horizontally across his chest. He hit the wall and the pole slipped up. It was against his neck suddenly. His eyes got big. I held the pole there, pushing the haft, pushing the basket. He let go of it but I didn't stop. I had him pinned against the wall, the pole across his throat. Desperately, he pummeled my body with both hands. I hardly felt it. When the blows began to weaken, I realized what I was doing. I sobbed and let go of the pole. Jack slid down the wall and sat down at its base with his head hanging, his breath wheezing asthmatically in his hurt throat. I stepped back and turned away from him, my legs trembling in reaction to what I had almost done.

Then I heard a noise. It was Jack scrambling to his feet. He still had some fight in him. He made a squawking noise in his throat and grabbed the ski pole, which had fallen near him. Before he could get up and swing it, Bunny reached him. I started to call her name. I never got it out. She had picked up one of the three-legged stools, swinging it by a leg. The edge of the seat struck Jack's head with a hard cracking sound. Bunny swung it again. This time the sound it made was soggy, like striking a ripe melon with the flat of a cleaver. Each time Bunny had struck with all her might.

She dropped the stool on the floor. It clattered and rolled a little and came to rest. "He tried to kill you!"

she cried. "He wanted to kill you...."

I went to Jack. He lay on his side with his legs drawn up. One of them twitched. I touched his head, above the ear on the right side where the stool had hit him. Through his hair it felt soft. There was not the expected resistance of hard bone. My fingers came away wet and red. Frantically I lifted his hand. I dug my fingers into his wrist, seeking the pulse. I felt a flutter, and another—then nothing.

Bunny looked at my face. I didn't have to say anything.

"Oh God," she said. "Oh God, no!"

She slid down slowly across Jack's legs, the back of her right hand to her mouth. Then I got all unwound. I don't really remember what I did next. I must have gotten dressed, for after a while I became aware of wearing my ski pants and shirt and sweater and windbreaker. I had even laced up my boots, and a lit cigarette was in my hand. Then I had to rush into the washroom, and I was sick there. I went outside and saw Jack's sled, the huskies hunkered down in their harnesses. The leader looked up at me, its fierce eyes like Bunny's, flat and blue. It yelped and a couple of the other dogs got to their feet but soon hunkered down again. The late afternoon wind had brought clouds up over the mountains and it looked as if it might snow before morning. Far away I heard a train whistle. One of the huskies howled an answer.

I went back inside. I didn't know what I was going to do yet. I could think of nothing except that Jack was inside there, dead. That we had fought and I had wanted to kill him for one wild moment and that Bunny had killed him.

I saw the phone on the counter. Call the hotel, I thought. Tell them we had a fight. They knew Jack was coming here to find me. They could call the sheriff's substation.

Bunny stood in the supply room doorway, her bare legs bent. She gripped the doorpost for support and said, "What are you going to do?" There was no color in her face at all.

"What the hell can I do?" I went to the phone. "Call the hotel."

"No, Chuck, wait a minute. Chuck." She came to me and her hand covered mine on the phone receiver. Her breasts were soft against my arm.

"We had a fight. I'll tell them. They don't have to know about you. You'll be all right."

"He had that pole. He was going to kill you. I had to. I had to do it."

"All right. You'll be all right. Let go of me. I want to call."

But she didn't take her hand away. "Chuck, listen to me."

"I've got to call."

"You've got to listen to me. Before he came, you said—remember?—you wanted to go away with me. It sounded crazy. I don't know, there are so many things. Like a beautiful dream, but—"

"He's in there," I shouted. "He's dead. He's not going to get up and walk off stage when the curtain drops. He's dead. We killed him."

"I'll go away with you, Chuck."

I smiled bitterly. "How far you think we'd get running?"

"We wouldn't have to run."

"They knew I was here. Knew he was coming here."

"Then get rid of him. We can do it."

I didn't look at her. I didn't want to see her face then I said: "Take a look outside."

"You won't call? Promise?"

"I'll wait."

She got into her ski pants and put on her galoshes and shoes. She went outside. She was gone a long time. I heard the huskies yelping. Then all of a sudden I heard a car engine start. It had never entered my head she'd leave me here holding the bag. I ran outside yelling.

She was getting out of the car. I could smell its exhaust. She had raced the motor, but it wasn't running now. I saw the sled—and the empty harnesses. I saw the last of the huskies scampering through the stand of pine this side of the advanced trail. I saw the footprints of the others.

"I took off their harnesses," she said. Her eyes were bright. That was the only change I had ever seen in them. "But still they wouldn't budge. I raced the motor to scare them. They're gone now."

I looked at the sled and the empty harnesses. "Break it down and burn it in the fireplace," Bunny said.

CHAPTER SIX

Suddenly it hit me. Inez had fired him. They had that argument about the dogs. Inez wouldn't pay for their transportation. He was mad enough to want to give us a hard time. He came to me, but I backed Inez up. He had a temper. Everybody knew it. He blew up and took off. Maybe he'd calm down later and send for the dogs. He was like that. He might have done it just like that—if he had lived.

Bunny was watching me. "I'll help you," she said.

I didn't want to think. I had this idea. It wasn't much, but I wanted to coast with it for a while.

Together we carried the big sled behind the lodge. Bunny took the blankets and cushions inside. The woodpile was covered over. I wrestled the sled up on the snowy pile it made and went into the supply room after the ax we split the logs with. Bunny had put more wood on the fire. She sat calmly in front of it with the two sled blankets, cutting them in strips with the big butcher knife she had found under the counter. When I went outside with the ax, she was feeding the first strip to the fire.

I hefted the ax and swung. It made a ringing hollow sound against the sled, and wood splintered. I thought they'd hear it clear down to Lake Placid. With every downward stroke of the ax I thought: not murder, but manslaughter. They'd get you for manslaughter. Or Bunny. Or both. What was it, ten to twenty years for manslaughter? Bunny behind bars, growing old there.

The ax rang on metal. Sparks flew. What was left of the sled slipped down off the snow-covered woodpile toward my feet. I chopped and pried the splintered wood away from the long, heavy runners.

Self-defense? I thought. They might believe it. Sometimes they did. He was a troublemaker. I could show them how he'd been a troublemaker. But wasn't it self-defense, anyhow, no matter what we did about it? He'd gone after the ski pole again. You could kill a man with that, couldn't you? You could....

I heard a car horn.

I dropped the ax and ran around the side of the lodge. A battered pre-war jalopy was parked behind Bunny's car and one of the Lake Placid teenagers who helped me with the ski slope got out. He didn't shut the door. A husky bounded out after him and he grabbed its collar, smiling at me, until it sat down in the snow.

"Say, I was driving up here to see if you needed a hand, Chuck," the boy said, "when this monster came running across the road. He's one of yours, isn't he?"

"Guess so."

"He must be. They're the only huskies around. Was Jack McCall up here with some of your guests or something?"

"No," I heard myself say. "He came up alone. We gave him the ax, Danny, and he wanted to see about shipping the dogs."

"No kidding! What happened?"

"He and Mrs. Cameron didn't get along so hot."

"Gee, that's too bad," Danny said, then asked: "You need some help? That's why I drove up."

"No, I don't think so, Danny, but thanks. I did about all I'm going to today. One of the hotel guests gave me a hand."

Danny looked at my face and grinned. "If those battle wounds mean anything, it must have been a lady guest."

That startled me. I didn't know what Danny was getting at for I didn't think Jack had marked me. I rubbed my cheek while Danny went on grinning. When I took my hand away, I saw a faint smear of lipstick on it.

Danny must have seen the look on my face, because he changed the subject quickly. "Well, not much light left anyhow," he said, gazing up at the slope and the rope tow which hadn't been touched.

"Maybe you can give us a hand tomorrow."

"Okay, swell. Should I leave the dog here with you?"

"Look, you want to do me a favor? Would you drop the dog off at the hotel for me and give Jack hell for letting it get loose?"

"Yeah, what the H, I'll take it back for you. If you

don't mind me picking up my girl first. She's crazy to see one of these monsters up close."

I said that would be fine and watched Danny coax the husky back into the car. Waving, he got in behind the wheel and shouted, "Wait till she gets a load of this monster."

"So long, Danny."

He backed the car up and swung it around, the chains crunching on snow. I watched him drive away and trudged back into the lodge. My mouth felt dry. It was hard to swallow. Just like that, I was in it.

Bunny came out of the supply room smoking a cigarette. "Who was that?"

"Just a kid who helps out around here. Don't worry, it's all right."

"What are you going to do now?"

She didn't look scared or worried or anything like that.

She had just come from the supply room, where Jack was.

She saw the way my eyes were looking and she said: "What could I do? You think I liked it? I had to go in there. I didn't know who it was."

"I'll bring the wood from the sled inside and burn it," I said.

"Chuck? Kiss me first."

She came squeezing against me and I kissed her hard enough to bruise her lips. At first I didn't feel anything, but all of a sudden it rocked me and she had to break away from me and step back. "I'll give you a hand," she said.

I went into the supply room to get an old tarp we had in there. I didn't look right at Jack's body, but I couldn't help seeing it. I started to feel queasy and hurried out with the tarp under my arm. Bunny came outside with me and we spread the tarp on the snow and piled all the wood we could find on it. I went down on hands and knees in the snow looking for any pieces we might have missed, then we folded the tarp over and took it inside and spread it out on top of the bearskin rug in front of the hearth. We chucked the splintered wood piece by piece into the fire.

"What happened to the runners?" Bunny asked me.

"I'll go get them."

"Yes, but then what?"

"I don't know yet."

"How soon will they start missing you at the hotel?"

"Not till dark. What about your husband?"

"He had a bottle at the motel. He's probably passed out by now."

"Bunny, do you really want to—go away with me?"

"Don't you? I love you, Chuck. It's crazy, but I love you."

"I mean, because we don't have to. We can fix this thing up so we don't have to run."

"Sure, of course. We're going to. What does that have to do with it?"

"Nothing. I don't know."

But I knew we had to have a reason for going away. With Jack missing too—assuming we could make it work out like that—we had to have a damn good reason. The best reason I could think of was the real one. That we were having an affair. We had to let them know we were having an affair.

"What about—him?" Bunny said.

We had the body. It hit me then. It came in waves. Sometimes I hardly thought about it at all, and then suddenly it hit me that the body was in there, that a little over an hour ago he had been alive and now he was dead. I went over to the counter and drank rum straight from the bottle, feeling its warmth spread in my belly. Bunny watched me drinking. I think maybe if she had put up a fuss about it then, like Inez, I still would have dropped the whole thing even if we already had implicated ourselves with the sled and with Danny. But she came over and said, "Save me a little, please."

I gave her the bottle. There was about an ounce left and she finished it off in two swallows. Her eyes got watery.

"Here's the thing," I said. "We can work it three ways. We either have to go about our business and get together later—"

"How much later?"

"I don't know how much. The second way," I said, ticking them off on my fingers but knowing even as I spoke that we'd have to tackle the immediate problem of the body before we did anything, "is just to take off without a word to anybody. But I don't like that, not if Jack McCall has to disappear too. It just might be tied together. The third way, we have to let our affair get around so we have a good reason for taking off—if you want to."

"No, I couldn't do it that way," she said quickly.

That surprised me. "Then you want to wait it out?"

"No, I—it wouldn't work that way either."

"Why not? You aren't making sense."

"I can't tell you why not."

"Oh, great! That's just great. Let's start keeping secrets."

"Isn't there any other way?"

"Sure. We can call the cops."

She looked away. When she spoke, it was to change the subject. "I hate him. I hate him, Chuck. You don't know what it's been like. Or maybe—why do you think

I was such a pushover?"

"Don't talk like that," I said. Then I thought of her coming out of Jack's cabin yesterday and tried to remember what kind of accusation Jack had flung at her here in the lodge when she slapped his face.

After a while she said, "Anyway, we can't do anything until—"

"Can you get away from him tonight?"

"Oh, am I going back?"

"You've got to, because I've got to get back to the hotel. I can't do anything until we're ready to put the guests to bed. It's Friday night. Plenty of things cooking at a resort hotel Friday night."

"I can get away tonight."

"Can you get away—afterwards?"

"Yes and no. Let's not talk about it till we have to. Trust me, Chuck. All right?"

"You don't give me much choice." I went over to the hearth and gathered up the tarp. I took it to the supply room and tossed it on the floor, then went out back for the sled runners. They were each about eight feet long and must have weighed ten or twelve pounds apiece. I brought then into the supply room and locked the door.

"That'll keep," I said. "I'm the only one who has the keys. Where are you staying?"

"Mirror Lake Motel. It's between Lake Placid and your hotel, on the main road."

"I know where it is. What unit?"

"The last one on the end away from the office. Do you have an idea about him?"

"Yeah."

"How long will it take?"

"I'll try to pick you up by two or two-thirty in the morning. Be ready outside. I'll try to get you back before it's light out."

"What are we going to do?"

"The only way to make him disappear living is to make him disappear dead."

"Yes, but how?"

"I'm working on it." I looked at my watch. It was almost a quarter to five. If I didn't get back to the hotel soon, they'd begin to wonder. "Come on, let's go."

We went outside together. The sky was darkening, and the wind blew flurries of snow off the drifts. I looked at the footprints and the ski trails going back and forth from the road to the lodge. They didn't tell any story as far as I could tell. But I didn't like the trails left by the huskies. I wondered if it would snow tonight.

"Chuck, hold me."

She came into my arms and I buried my head in her hair, the wind whipping it about my face, "I don't want to keep secrets from you," she said. "Maybe later I can—"

"Okay."

"It's going to work out for us, Chuck."

"Yeah. Two o'clock. Be ready outside."

I watched her get into her car. The starter ground cold and weak, but turned over on the third try. She pulled out in reverse and made a U-turn and drove down the road. I climbed into the four-wheel drive station wagon and swung it around. Except for the stool with her fingerprints on it, she was in the clear now. If she didn't show up at two o'clock, I could hardly blame her. Then I thought, what's the matter with you? You're in love with each other, aren't you?

I drove down to the highway and back to the hotel.

CHAPTER SEVEN

"Chuck? I see you a minute?"

It was Elaine Skinner. She saw me come in the door and waved to me. In slacks and a canary yellow sweater, she stood near the desk with a man I had never seen before. He was a big fellow, about my age or a couple of years older. He was dressed as if he'd just come from the city, in a dark gray suit and a snap-brim hat. He carried a tweed overcoat folded on his arm. He was a pretty solid-looking guy, with the calm self-assurance on his face that women usually eat up. I walked over to them. I don't know why, but I was wary.

"This is our Mr. Odlum," Elaine told him. "Maybe he can help you."

"It's either him or the bar, or I draw another blank," the man said with a little smile. "I've tried everyone else."

"What's up?" I said. "How can I help you?"

"Police investigation, Mr. Odlum." He took out his wallet and flipped it open to show me the shield pinned inside. He put the wallet away and reached into his pocket for a glossy photograph.

"You ever see this man?"

I held my face rigid. My heart began to pound. It was a head and shoulders snap, like a passport photo, of Orin Kemp. A number on a black rectangle over his chest ran across the bottom of the picture. Orin Kemp wasn't smiling. He was staring straight at the camera, dead serious.

I needed time to think. I didn't want the police finding Orin Kemp now, whatever they wanted him for. I tried to remember what had happened yesterday. The bar, I thought suddenly. He'd gone in there for a drink. Sammy might recognize him. I pretended to study the picture.

"Well?"

"This is one of those mug shots, isn't it?"

"Hardly. The man's a taxi driver in New York. Company photo."

"No, I don't think I've ever seen him before. But I haven't been at the hotel all day."

"Could have been yesterday. Here's the way it is, Mr. Odlum: I was following him late yesterday afternoon, but my car got stuck in a snowbank in Lake Placid. He was driving this way, so I've been checking all the hotels."

"He could have driven through to Saranac Lake. The road ends there."

"So I've been told. Then you don't recognize him?"

"No. Sorry."

"Guess I'll try the bar."

I took the picture out of his hand. "Here, let me do it for you," I said.

He looked at me, then shrugged. "Sure, why not?"

I took the snapshot into the bar. Sammy was serving beer to a couple of guests. When I sat down at the bar I could see the cop out of the corner of my eye, standing in the doorway.

"Hiya, Chuck. How's the snow man?"

"Great." I put my arm on the bar with the picture cupped in my hand. "You got any of that imported Danish beer left?" I asked softly. I knew we'd run out of that beer earlier in the week.

"Come again?" Sammy leaned toward me over the bar because I hadn't spoken loud enough for him to hear. It would look as if he leaned over for a closer scrutiny of the picture.

"You got any of that imported Danish beer left?" I asked again.

Sammy shook his head. "Nope. Clean out."

"Okay, thanks. I'll order some from the distributor."

"Anything else?"

"No. Sorry to bother you, Sammy."

"That's what I'm here for."

I went back to the cop.

"No luck?"

I shook my head. "Never saw him before in his life." I handed him the picture. "Sorry we couldn't help you. What's he wanted for?"

"Police investigation. Well, I'll be shoving off."

I walked him into the lobby and he put on his coat and nodded and left. All of a sudden it socked me! I wondered when he'd get around to the Mirror Lake Motel.

"What's the beef?" I asked Elaine.

"I was curious too, but you know cops. I couldn't get to first base."

"Well, it doesn't matter."

The evening and night stretched out over an arctic tundra of time. I thought of Jack McCall's body up there in the lodge, waiting. I thought of Bunny and knew we might have to take off in a hurry after all, because sooner or later the cop would get around to Mirror Lake. But why was he looking for Orin Kemp? And if the worst happened, if he found him, what would it mean to Bunny? What would Bunny do?

What I wanted more than anything right now was a chance to sack out, for we were in for a busy night. I went upstairs after dinner and stretched out on the bed, but I was strung too tight for sleep.

This time of year, I thought, Whiteface Lake and

Mirror Lake would be frozen solid. For the past month we'd been running toboggans down the chute across the street from the hotel and onto the ice of Whiteface Lake. Placid was bigger and deeper, but not big enough. A sheet of ice a foot thick would cover it. That left Lake Champlain, about forty miles away. It was big and deep and the water ran very swift near Port Kent south of Plattsburg. Ice all the way across? I didn't know. I had driven into Plattsburg last week to see about a Poma lift for the ski slope, and the fishing shacks had already been up on the ice of the lake. But some winters it never froze all the way across till late February. And if it had, what then? I didn't want to think about that. I didn't have any answer to it. Because Jack McCall was going to disappear tonight, and disappearing meant sinking his body in the night-black water of Lake Champlain.

About a quarter to ten, Inez came into the room. "Oh, there you are. Aren't you going to change?"

I was still wearing my ski clothes. "No," I said. "This is my drumming-up-trade costume."

"But it's Friday night. If we expect the guests to dress for the weekend—"

"No skiing today. I have to sign them up from scratch for tomorrow."

"Sprawled out on the bed?"

I got up. "Don't worry, Inez. I'll handle my end."

"Meaning I won't handle mine?"

"I didn't say that."

"But you implied it."

"Look, if you're nothing else you're efficient. You do your job."

"You make that sound like a criticism too."

"If you think I imply you're not efficient, that's a criticism. If I say you are efficient, that's criticizing too. What do you want me to say?"

"Nothing. Nothing at all."

"Anyhow, it's your hotel."

"Have I ever thrown that in your face? You'd think I was guilty of some kind of crime just owning the Whiteface."

"I'm going downstairs," I said.

"Chuck, why do we always have to fight? I want us to get along. I try."

"Okay, forget it," I snapped.

"You draw enough money, don't you?"

Most of the profits Inez plowed back into the hotel. In the spring she wanted to build more cottages for the summer trade. I had no living expenses, of course, but I drew fifty a week for pocket money. It was plenty and I said so.

"Then what is it? Do you want that Poma lift very badly?"

"Costs thirty-five hundred installed," I said.

"That's a lot of money."

"I know. Maybe next year."

She went over to the bed. "Chuck, I'm sorry for being cross with you. You want to—give me a back message? We have time."

I looked at her. She had that way of saying it. She wanted me to make love to her. Like the special childhood words for bodily functions.

"I better get downstairs and sign them up," I said.

She didn't say anything to stop me. I socialized around for a couple of hours, signing up beginning and intermediate skiers for tomorrow's lessons. Just before midnight I went to the main entrance and looked out. It had begun to snow. I went into the bar and had a drink. One of the waiters was helping Sammy out with the Friday night business.

"Evening, Mr. Odlum."

I saw the cop who had showed me Orin Kemp's picture.

"Any luck?"

"Unfortunately, no. I'm staying here overnight. Nice place you have."

I bought him a drink and asked, "Be trying Saranac Lake in the morning, or what?"

"Couple of motels down the road I still have to hit. Then it's Saranac Lake, I guess."

"Why don't you catch the show in the nightclub? The boys really go to town Friday nights. A western routine."

"Maybe I'll do that."

"Well, here's how."

"Mud in your eye."

We had our drinks and I got out of there. A couple of motels down the road. Including the one at Mirror Lake? I sat down behind the desk and took out my wallet. I had thirty-three dollars and change on me. You couldn't get very far on that. There might be a couple of hundred in cash and endorsed checks in the hotel safe, more if Kirby Rowe hadn't driven down to the bank in Lake Placid this afternoon. I figured I'd have a look before leaving.

Wally and his four-piece combo called it a night at a quarter to two. But someone, one of the guests probably, was still beating out tunes on the piano in the nightclub. Sammy was mopping up in the bar. "What a night!" he said. "Don't they ever sleep?"

By two-fifteen the only one left in the lobby was Andy Dahlgren, the night deskman. But I could hear voices coming from the lounge and the nightclub.

"Why don't you grab a beer before Sammy closes up?" I suggested. "I'll hold down the fort."

"Thanks a lot, Chuck."

When he was gone I looked into the PBX room. It was dark and empty. I looked around the lobby. No one there. I sat on my heels in front of the safe and spun the dial. Twice past zero to the right, fifteen. Once around to the left, twenty-six. Then right three. I swung the door, working very quickly, pushing aside half a dozen deposit envelopes that held valuables belonging to some of the guests. Behind them I found the cash drawer and took it out.

There was more money than I had thought. Over three hundred in bills and almost five hundred more in endorsed checks. I decided to leave the checks alone: cashing them on the run we could be traced. I stuffed the bills in my pocket and put the cash drawer away. When I shut the safe I heard footsteps. I got up and swung around.

"Oh, there you are," Kirby Rowe said. "I've been meaning to have a talk with you all night."

I wondered if I had a guilty look on my face. But what the hell, I thought, I had a perfect right to go to the safe.

"You see McCall at the lodge?" Kirby asked.

"Yeah, he came up there."

"Before dinner a town kid brought one of his dogs in. We got a call from the Marcy in Lake Placid a couple of hours ago. One of McCall's dogs was kicking their garbage cans around."

"I'll be damned," I said.

"What happened up there this afternoon?"

"I guess you were right about him, Kirby. He came in yelling how we were going to pay to ship his dogs or else."

"Yes? What did you tell him?"

"The same thing I told him yesterday. That it would

come out of his severance pay."

"He didn't like it?"

"That's putting it mildly."

"Well, he hasn't shown up since. What I want to know is how those dogs got loose."

"Maybe he was mad enough to turn them loose. He's an employee of the hotel. If there's any trouble, we're responsible."

"Don't you think that's going to extremes?"

I shrugged. "You called the ticket on him, Kirby. I wouldn't put anything past him."

Then Kirby said just what I'd wished he'd say. "What about the rest of the dogs—if he doesn't come back at all?"

"You mean if he just left them? For good?"

"That's what I mean, yes. If he turned one team loose already ..." Kirby spread his hands out. "We don't even know how to feed them."

"We can call the vet in Lake Placid in the morning if he hasn't shown up by then. Hasn't he called or anything?"

Kirby Rowe shook his head.

"The son of a bitch," I said.

Kirby's grin was bleak. "It took you long enough to learn how irresponsible he really is."

"I guess I owe you an apology."

"Forget it. I'll call the vet in the morning unless Mrs. Cameron can think of something else."

"I'll ask her, but what else can we do?"

"Search me. Well, good night, Chuck."

"Night, Kirby." He went across the lobby and upstairs.

In a few minutes Andy Dahlgren came back. "Really hit the spot," he said. "Turning in?"

"No. I think I'll batten down the hatches."

I had left my windbreaker in the cloakroom outside the lounge. Wearing it over a flannel shirt and a sweater, it was all I needed for skiing. For what we had to do tonight it wouldn't be warm enough, but I didn't want to go upstairs for something else because Inez would be in bed by now.

Outside, I kicked over the Willys wagon and let the engine warm. I crossed the street and went down the steps to the toboggan chute. The wind blew so hard across the lake you couldn't tell what was fresh snow falling and what was snow whipped off the drifts. I picked up one of the small one-man toboggans and banged the snow off it on the side of the chute. I brought it back to the station wagon, dragging it across the snow by the tow rope. Would I need anything else? A flashlight, I thought, and some strong wire. I found a flashlight in the garage and tried it. The beam was bright. With its help I found a spool of insulated wire on the shelf above where the skis were stored. I tried to break it between my hands but couldn't. It was strong enough. Anything else? Yes—I couldn't do it alone. There was something else. Bunny.

Suddenly I wanted to see her. It didn't matter what I had to do tonight, I wanted to see her anyway.

On the way over to Mirror Lake I caught the two-thirty newscast on the five-minute break of an all-night disc jockey show. The French were getting their lumps in North Africa, the commentator said. They were getting another satellite ready on the pad at Cape Canaveral, he said. The Adirondacks region was due for its worst snow storm in six years, he predicted. Two-thirty-five. I shut the radio off. I'd be late. Would Bunny still wait—if she'd waited at all?

The headlights carved two yellow tunnels in the falling snow, the snow dancing in them like golden confetti. I lit a cigarette and realized my hands were shaking. At a quarter to three I went up the driveway of the Mirror Lake Motel. It was a small place, eight attached units in red brick with an office and a small restaurant at one end. There was no sign to say it was approved by any of the auto clubs.

When I pulled up in front of the last unit I heard her footsteps crunching on the snow. I leaned over and opened the door and she was sitting next to me. Then she came into my arms. My elbow hit the horn ring and it gave a loud blast before I could get off it.

"Jesus," I said. I started to drive, still holding her with one hand. She was shaking like a leaf.

"I'm half frozen," she said, her teeth chattering. "I waited and waited. I thought you weren't going to come."

"Any trouble?"

"He's asleep."

"Won't he worry if he gets up and you're not there?"

"He's a sound sleeper. And he can take care of his worries."

"What's that supposed to mean?"

"Not now, Chuck."

We drove in silence along Route 86. In the darkness, I almost missed the turnoff. I braked hard and the four-wheel-drive kept us from skidding.

"I'm freezing. I wish I had something to drink."

"Scared?"

"I ought to be." She squeezed my arm. "But not with you, Chuck."

"Here we are." I cut the headlights but left the motor running. I got out and opened the tail gate and pulled the toboggan down on the snow.

She was standing next to me. "What's that for?" Then it hit her. "Oh, Chuck...."

We stood there a minute with the toboggan between us. "Come on. We've got a lot of driving to do."

I pulled the toboggan tow rope and started walking through the snow toward the lodge. Wind whipped the falling snow against my face. I felt numb. I knew what had to be done and I wanted to go through the motions without thinking. When we reached the lee of the lodge I said, "Damn, wait a minute." I gave Bunny the tow rope and went back to the Willys for the flashlight.

"Here."

I gave Bunny the flashlight and opened the door. We went inside together, leaving the door open. My ski boots clattered on the floor. The flashlight made a yellow circle on the floor, on the bearskin rug, finally on the supply room door. I fumbled for the key and opened the door. The light leaped across the little room to the posters on the wall.

"Get it down," I said.

Then suddenly the light was on Jack McCall's mackinaw. He lay as he had fallen, on his side with his knees drawn up. I crouched and forced him over on his back. His knees remained up. His body had stiffened. Bunny made a small frightened sound, but the flashlight remained steady.

I got him into a sitting position and draped both his arms over my left shoulder. They wouldn't bend right. I stood up straight and lifted him. For a moment I stood balancing his weight in a fireman's carry, looking down at the pool of yellow light at my feet. Then I took a step and caught one ski boot on the rumpled tarp. I went two steps toward the door, regaining my balance. One of his arms thumped against my back, hard and stiff like wood. I went through the doorway sideways. His legs caught there anyway, and I had to turn to get them free.

"Aren't you going to lock up?"

"Not yet."

Bunny led the way outside. All of a sudden it wasn't Jack McCall I had to carry. It was just a stiff heavy weight on my shoulders and sticks thumping my back. It was just something I had to carry. Anything, you name it.

I set it down on the toboggan. The legs hung over the side and I straightened them. I pulled it across the snow to the station wagon and wrestled it up from the toboggan and over the tail gate. I eased it down on the floor. Then for a minute it was Jack McCall again, with snow in his red hair.

"Get the goddamn light off him," I said harshly.

"I'm sorry."

"Back in a minute."

I walked into the lodge again to take care of the rest of it. Bunny came halfway with me. "Here, you'll need this."

She gave me the flashlight.

CHAPTER EIGHT

I couldn't find any blood on the floor. I took the stool Bunny had hit him with to the sink behind the counter and washed it off, running my hand hard on the edge of the seat. Then I brought it back to the supply room, examining the floor again and finding nothing. I picked up the tarp and the two heavy sled runners, locked the door and went outside. I put the runners in the back of the station wagon across his body, then spread the tarp over him. Chances were a thousand to one against being stopped, but if we were, the runners under the tarp broke the contours of his body.

We climbed into the front of the station wagon without talking. Bunny lit two cigarettes and gave me one. For a minute I just sat there smoking. I looked at my hands. They were steady. Bunny was fidgeting with the zipper grip on her windbreaker, running it up and down the little metal teeth.

"Where are we going?"

"Lake Champlain."

"Isn't that a long way?"

"Forty miles."

I started to drive.

It took us an hour and fifteen minutes to go forty miles through the snow. We drove, down out of the mountains on Route 86, passing through the silent main streets of Wilmington and Jay. At Ausable Forks we took 9N to Keeseville and Ausable Chasm. By then it was snowing harder—a lucky break, I thought, for any tracks we left would be covered before daylight. It was twenty after four when we reached Port Kent on Lake Champlain.

I drove up the main drag to the municipal dock, then turned left along the frozen shore of the lake. Pretty soon I found what I wanted, a road going off into one of Port Kent's several deserted summer bungalow colonies. Boards covered the windows of the one-story clapboard buildings. One thing I hadn't counted on was the snow, because plows hadn't come through here. I gave myself a bad time thinking of what would happen if we got stuck, but the four-wheel-drive kept us moving.

The road ended at the edge of the frozen lake. I pulled up and got out without giving myself time to think. I opened the tail gate and climbed inside and passed the toboggan out to Bunny. Then I removed the tarp and threw the runners out on the snow. Grabbing the body by its shoulders, I dragged it toward the tail gate, let it go and climbed down.

Bunny helped me ease it out. We pulled it past its point of balance and let it fall. One shoulder struck the toboggan heavily, but the legs trailed off on the snow. Bunny sobbed. She turned away for a minute while I straightened the body on the toboggan.

"I—I'm all right now."

I didn't say anything. I went back to the front seat of the station wagon for the insulating wire. At first I couldn't find it. That's great, I thought, knowing it wouldn't take much of that to make me go all unstrung. The wire had slid down to the rear of the seat, between the seat and the backrest. I found it there.

Bunny watched while I secured the two runners, one to Jack McCall's arm and one to his leg. Between them they weighed twenty-five pounds, I thought, and the water was cold. Twenty-five pounds would be enough. I used all the wire, wrapping it around and around an arm and a leg and both runners and securing it with knots.

"Ice," Bunny said almost hysterically. "It's all ice."

"I don't think so. Let's go."

I pulled the toboggan. It came smoothly across the snow and we went down with it across the snow-covered beach.

There was a little incline leading down to the lake. Then everything was flat and I knew we were on the lake itself. In five minutes we passed the first fishing shack. It was about the size of an outhouse and loomed dark against the falling snow. We kept going, straight out from shore over the snow and the ice beneath it. We passed four more fishing shacks in the next few minutes. I didn't like that. It meant the ice was solid. All the way across?

My legs felt like lead and the tow rope began to tug at my shoulder sockets. I was breathing hard. I stopped for a minute, but Bunny went on ahead. In a little while she came running back, excited.

"Water," she said. "I can hear it."

We went on another five minutes. There were no more fishing shacks. There was only the falling snow and the flat white surface of the frozen lake.

Then I heard it. Water rushing turbulently somewhere ahead of us.

In another few minutes we saw it. The snow-covered ice ended ahead of us, as if it had been cut off with shears. Beyond it, lapping and swirling, was black water. When we got close I could see chunks of ice floating in it.

"Watch your step," I said. "Ice is liable to be thin."

I pulled the toboggan to within a few feet of the edge. I heard the ice creak underfoot.

"Hurry up, I'm numb," Bunny said, her teeth chattering again.

She helped me roll the body off the toboggan, then stepped back. I rolled it over twice more, the runners like splints on an arm and a leg. Then all of a sudden I heard the ice crack. I did the only thing I could. I jumped back.

It was a nightmare. It couldn't be happening, but it was. The thin shelf of ice at the edge cracked. It swayed and dipped, and water washed over it, drenching the body. Then, breaking completely free, it bobbed and began to float away in the dark current. With the body right in the middle of it.

"Oh God, Chuck...."

I sat down and tugged frantically at the laces of my

ski boots. Outer laces first, then the inner laces. I flung the boots away and stood up. The slab of ice with Jack's body on it caught in an eddy and turned slowly around. It was already about five yards out.

I ran and dove and hit the water flat. I heard Bunny cry out. What I expected was terrible numbing cold. What I felt was a wall of fire with a million stinging needles in it. Hitting flat in a surface dive, I had lost my breath. I didn't get it back. The water was too cold to feel cold. It burned.

On fire with it, but numb too, I swam. I knew I had to hurry. I couldn't last more than a couple of minutes.

My head hit the shelf of ice. The ice bobbed. It was only a few inches thick, with a foot of snow on top of it. I got my arms out of the water and tried to pull myself up. I couldn't make it. Gasping, I went under. On my next try I got my arms and chest on the ice. Then I began sliding back. I grabbed something. It was Jack's arm, the one without the runner. I went under again, holding it. When I broke surface again the body had slid to the edge of the ice. The arm dangled off it. Still holding it, I went under a third time.

All at once I felt the weight. It was in the water with me. I let go and came to the surface. The chunk of ice floated away. It was just ice.

I turned and tried to swim. Swallowed a lot of water and heard Bunny's voice urging me. I didn't think I was getting anywhere. I wanted to relax and let myself go. Then I felt Bunny's hands. The sharp broken edge of the ice cut across my chest as Bunny tugged at my shoulders, her voice urging but the words without meaning in the wind and wet cold.

Then I lay on the ice.

"Come on, get up. You'll freeze. Get up, please."

That was when the cold really hit me. I trembled all over. I said something, I don't know what. I got to my knees, then Bunny grasped my elbow and I was standing. She held my arm. The wind blew behind us as we started to walk.

"... I do it?"

"Yes. He's in the water. He went down. Keep moving."

We walked. I don't remember how far, but it seemed to take a long time. When we stopped I heard a noise. Metal striking metal. Bunny was using the butt of the flashlight on the padlock and hasp of one of the fishing shacks.

Then the door swung, creaking, and she helped me inside. It was deliciously warm in there, without the wind, without the snow, without the cold, killing night.

I heard a scratching, and a match flared. Bunny found a kerosene lantern, lit it. It glowed orange against the corrugated tin walls of the shack and the single window covered with glazed paper. There were shelves with fishing tackle on them, and a pile of magazines. Two pairs of fatigue trousers hung from their belt loops on a hook behind the door. Next to them hung a faded flannel shirt.

"Get undressed," Bunny said.

My fingers were so stiff with cold that I couldn't even unzip my windbreaker. Bunny did it for me and peeled away the jacket coated with ice. She worked swiftly and efficiently, then, undressing me. I stood staring at the canvas camp chair and the round fishing hole in the middle of the ice floor. I began to feel cold again. I couldn't stop shaking.

Bunny came to me, wrapping her arms around me. She must have felt the shaking. "We've got to get you warm," she said. Then she went away. I shut my eyes and stumbled toward the camp chair, but she grabbed my arm. "Stay on your feet, Chuck."

She'd taken the flannel shirt down from its hook and began to rub me with it. She rubbed and rubbed, all over. It made a leathery scraping sound. It felt like sandpaper.

"All right, sit down."

She went to work on my legs. I looked down at her blond hair, damp from the snow. My arms and shoulders and chest had begun to tingle and I wasn't shaking so bad now.

"Here, put it on." She gave me the shirt and I got into it. She brought a pair of the khaki pants over, and I put them on and stood up.

My own clothing was in a pile on the floor. Without thinking, I stuffed it down the fishing hole. At the time it seemed like the thing to do. The windbreaker hung there for a moment, then was swept away.

"What about my boots?"

"I've got them right here."

I put them on and sat down again. Lacing them for me, Bunny said, "I shoved the toboggan in the water. Will it sink?"

"Probably. It doesn't matter. You're sure he went down?"

"I saw him go down."

"We did it, baby."

"We did it." Bunny touched my knee. "It's after five o'clock. We have to get going, don't we? What time does it get light around here?"

"Not for another hour and a half." I had stopped shaking, but my face felt numb. The words came out in choppy, frozen phrases. I said, "A cop came around the Whiteface yesterday looking for your husband."

"A cop?"

"Yeah. He had a picture. He said your husband drove

a hack in New York."

"That's right. Describe him to me, the cop."

"Big guy. Around thirty or a little older. Regular features, pretty good-looking. He looked very confident and sure of himself. Had a deep voice. He said he'd be checking a couple of motels down the road in the morning."

"The Mirror Lake?"

"Maybe, I don't know."

"A tall man, even taller than you, with broad shoulders and dark hair?"

"He wore a hat. It sounds like the same guy. You know him?"

"So he's here," Bunny said, more to herself than to me.

"You know him? I thought he was a cop."

"Are you all right now?"

I said I was all right.

"Then let's get out of here. I've got to get back."

"Are we sticking together, Bunny? Or what?"

"Do you have to ask me?"

"You were kind of evasive about it yesterday."

"Kiss me, Chuck. Kiss me hard."

I kissed her and her arms came around me. Her heart beat against my ribs. Our lips parted just enough for her to talk and she said, "I'm sticking with you, Chuck. All the way. I couldn't help stalling yesterday. I had to know what you'd do. I had to wait till—afterwards."

"What is it? What about the cop?"

"I'll tell you in the car."

I wanted to kiss her again, but she drew away from me. Something was riding her, riding her hard. She turned the lantern down, and we went out together into the wind and snow. She didn't wait to shut the door. She started running. What had happened tonight? I thought. Had that got to her all of a sudden? I didn't think so; I thought it was something else. The cop? I started running after her. All I was wearing was the flannel shirt, about two sizes too small for me, tight khaki pants and my ski boots. I got the shakes again before I reached the dark bungalow colony on its little rise above the beach, but the heater in the station wagon would take care of that.

Bunny had started the motor, for I'd left the ignition key in its lock. I shut the tail gate and climbed in under the wheel. I turned the Willys around and took 9N west out of Port Kent, not talking. I was waiting for her to open up. She sat stiffly and stared straight ahead. We went on like that, without a word, until we reached Keeseville. My face and hands had begun to sting with frostbite. I had no feeling in my toes at all.

Finally Bunny said, her voice very soft and even, "He's got a lot of money, Chuck. My husband."

That was about the last thing I'd expected. "Yeah? So what?"

"That's why I couldn't just go away. It's also why I couldn't tell him I wanted to leave him for another man. He wouldn't have believed me."

I didn't say anything.

"Besides, I wouldn't go away—without the money."

"Lay off that," I said. "That's looking for trouble."

"With him, Chuck. There in the motel. More money than—"

"Lay off it!" I said savagely. I didn't know what was the matter with her.

"Money that he couldn't report stolen or missing or anything."

"It's hot, is that what you mean? Is that what the cop's after?"

"That money could be ours, Chuck. Yours and mine."

"Forget it. We're either clearing out or we're not. I wouldn't stick my neck out. Listen, Bunny. I took the day's cash out of the safe at the Whiteface. It's over three hundred—" Then I remembered. I'd thrown that money down the hole in the ice in the fishing shack. "Forget it," I said. "I lost it."

Bunny started laughing. It went on and on and she couldn't control it. I took my eyes off the road to look at her. Tears were running down her cheeks.

"Cut it out," I said.

"What did you lose, three hundred dollars? Oh, Chuck, Chuck...." She was still laughing.

It was as if she were crazy. Suddenly I wanted to hit her. I wanted to make her stop. I shouted, "How much does your husband have—a grand? Two grand? Five? Well, even if it were ten grand I'd say forget it. We'll make out. And stop your damn laughing." After a while the laughter subsided. I stared at the road and the snow rushing at the headlights. I listened to the swish-thump, swish-thump of the windshield wipers. I said, "We were lucky. We're out of it, but we were lucky. That could change. We can't go messing around with any money your husband's got. Especially since that cop's after it. Well, isn't he?"

She didn't deny it. She didn't say anything. I thought of her playing up to Jack McCall, and the bottom dropped out of everything. I asked her: "How long have you planned on getting away from him—with the money? About as long as you knew Jack McCall?"

"Chuck—"

"Then what happened?" I lashed out at her. "Did you think you found a bigger sucker than Jack McCall? Was he afraid to touch it? Is that why—"

"Chuck, please. I was only laughing because you

looked so solemn about that three hundred dollars. Three hundred dollars. I was all wound up. I couldn't help it."

They were words. Just words. I hardly heard them. I felt a sickening feeling, like a blow to the stomach. I had to grip the wheel hard to keep the station wagon from swerving. "Wait a minute," I said. "Wait a minute! You picked up the stool. You hit him with it. He was already out. He couldn't have hurt us, but he knew. He knew what you wanted, didn't he, Bunny? You hit him because you couldn't let him go on knowing since you'd found a bigger sucker. You meant to kill him. You wanted to kill him."

I looked at her. She had turned in the seat to face me. She didn't bother denying it. She licked her lips. Her eyes were blue glass behind her narrowed lids. All she said was:

"Chuck. My husband has a hundred and seventeen thousand dollars, Chuck."

CHAPTER NINE

All night the strain and the tension had mounted in her, but she'd kept herself from flying apart until now by sheer will power. What else could I think?

"Sure," I said. "A hundred and seventeen thousand dollars."

"Don't you believe me?"

Maybe I should have humored her, but eating away at the back of my mind was the fact that Jack McCall had picked up an option on this crazy business before I had, and now he was dead, and in a way I had been used to kill him and get rid of the body. "Okay, your husband has some money," I said. "Though what the hell he's doing with it up here in the middle of the winter, that I can't figure out. And as for the amount, I stopped believing in fairy tales a long time ago."

We drove through Jay and up into the high mountains with the first pale pre-dawn light. Howling, the wind funneled down through the passes and buffeted the station wagon, driving the snow before it in blinding swirls of white. I had to lean forward and wipe condensed moisture off the windshield.

"You're a real nut," Bunny said. "First you accuse me of all sorts of things, up to and including murder, then you refuse to believe the only reason for all of it that would make sense." She added, almost indignantly: "What's the matter with you? Which is it? Because either—"

"All right, let's take it one thing at a time. What's your husband doing up here in the mountains with a hundred and—what was it?—a hundred and seventeen thousand bucks?"

"You don't know him. He's a fool. He's got a wild idea of going up to Canada. Don't you think I tried to talk him out of it? Because he can't even start spending that kind of money in Canada in American currency, or in any currency at all for that matter, without arousing suspicion. He wouldn't listen to me, that's all. And we had to leave separately so it wouldn't look like we were running out. That's why I was waiting for him up here."

"No man who can grab himself that kind of dough would be such a fool, Bunny. Try again."

"No? Sometimes I think *all* men are fools. Now will you at least let me tell it to you from the beginning without any interruptions? Unless of course you don't have any interest at all in a hundred and seventeen thousand dollars."

"Go ahead, I'm listening." Any minute now I expected her to admit it was really just a couple of thousand bucks that her husband had.

"You remember the Teddy Walling kidnapping case?"

"Sure I remember it, but don't make me laugh. The confessed kidnappers were tried and found guilty and condemned to death. Maybe they've already been executed, I don't know. So don't go telling me your husband was involved in that." But even as I spoke the memory of the newspaper stories on the Teddy Walling kidnapping case began to nibble at my mind. The Walling kid, who had lived in Manhattan, had been snatched from a private school in the East Seventies. Later it had come out that the kidnappers had driven up into Putnam County with him, shot him to death within two hours of taking him, and buried the body. They gave the parents—Walling was a TV company executive, I remembered—a rough time for a week, pretending the kid was still alive, insisting on a ransom somewhere in the neighborhood of a quarter of a million bucks. The ransom had been paid, and though Walling was rich it had taken almost a week to get it together, for the kidnappers had insisted on small bills not in series. And suddenly I remembered something else; the details were fuzzy in my mind, but though the kidnappers had been captured, less than half of the ransom money had been recovered.

"As a matter of fact, they're in the death house at Sing Sing awaiting execution," Bunny told me. "But that's beside the point. Do you remember anything about the kidnappers?"

"A little. His name was—let me see—Sloan, wasn't it? Mickey Sloan. Her name was Hannah something."

"Hannah Howard. Go on."

"Well, from what I recall, they were a couple of lushes. Not married, but living together, dreaming the whole scheme up over a couple of years, drinking three fifths a day between them and telling each other what big brave brilliant people they were and how it wasn't right they had to scrounge around for a buck all their lives. Then, amazingly, they stayed sober long enough to pull it off like clockwork, but I don't remember the details."

"Hannah Howard picked the Walling boy up at school, telling the teacher she was Mr. Walling's sister and that her brother had just come down with a stroke or something."

"The kid went along with that?"

"It was a nursery school. Teddy Walling was only three."

"Then they got picked up within twenty-four hours after getting the money, didn't they?"

"That's right. They were still a couple of lushes, as you put it, and a few days couldn't change that. They remained sober only long enough to handle the ransom details. By then the cops were in on it, of course, and the FBI. Because under the new laws the FBI can come in within twenty-four hours. But the FBI never advises about the ransom money. That is, the parents have to decide whether they think it will help get their child back and the FBI goes along with their decision."

"Walling decided to pay?"

"Yes, he did. A friend of the family had to deliver the money twice, without police or FBI interference. The first time, nobody showed up for it. Later, knowing what Sloan and Hannah Howard were like, the police assumed they were drunk the first time. Anyhow, the second time the money was dropped, they picked it up. A quarter of a million dollars, Chuck, in small bills out of series. And, as you say, success was too much for Sloan and Hannah Howard. Less than a day later they went on a wild bender, and the police got them. Do you remember how it happened? It was in the papers."

I was suddenly cold all over, and it had nothing to do with the ducking. For I remembered how the police had caught Sloan and Hannah Howard. It was in all the papers, and with that kind of money involved in a kidnapping case, they'd made a big thing of it, splashing headlines over all the front pages for a week. Sloan and Hannah Howard had been fingered by a taxi driver.

"You better tell me," I said. My voice was unsteady.

"Well, later the friend of the Walling family told the FBI how he had delivered the money. A quarter of a million dollars in small bills is a lot of paper. He had stuffed it into a tan cowhide two-suiter, a small duffle and a gladstone bag. They were dropped under a culvert in Westchester at the appointed time. Sloan and the Howard woman picked up all three bags. They admitted that to the police later. But when they were taken, all the cops found on them was the two-suiter—with ninety thousand dollars in it. Ninety thousand, out of a quarter of a million. That was in the papers too."

We passed through Wilmington in bleak gray daylight and turned south on Route 86. A car going the other way passed us, laboring slowly uphill through the fresh snow. I drove by reflex action. Filled to bursting with Bunny's story, I couldn't think of anything else.

"Let's go back a ways," she said. "Sloan and Hannah Howard picked up the ransom money and drove on up to Putnam County. They had a house there, near Lake Mahopac. Sloan was a handyman and gardener who earned most of his money from the summer tourists on the lake. That was where they buried the boy's body, by the way, right in their own backyard. Afterwards, they led the cops to the grave and they found him there. But one thing they insisted on all along, not that it mattered or did them any good: they didn't know what had happened to the missing hundred and sixty thousand dollars. The police and the FBI never found it, Chuck. It's still missing."

"So I gathered."

Bunny laughed. "Speaking of gathering, you haven't accused me of any woolgathering the last few minutes."

"Go ahead with it, will you?"

"Well, there isn't much more to tell. Sloan and the Howard woman were telling the truth about the missing money, though. They didn't know what happened to it. They didn't know because they were stewed to the gills when it was taken from them. The day after they got the money, they took the New York Central down to the city and had themselves a ball. They had been strung tight for a week and both of them were compulsive drinkers. Also, they knew they were in the clear, because nothing they had done could tie them to the kidnapping. Down in New York, probably dreaming alcoholically how they were going to spend all that money, they really let themselves go.

"They picked up a cab at Grand Central and hit a few night spots. They never let the cab go. The driver stayed with them, outside, while they did their drinking. After just the first place they were pretty high. At the second place they tossed a ten spot at the cabbie and told him to wait. He waited, all right. Wild horses couldn't have driven him away.

"After the second spot, they began to boast about all the money they had. They had given him another ten to prove it, and the evening was still young. They asked him to hang around, and he didn't need any coaxing."

"The cabbie was your husband?"

"Sure, of course. By the time they hit the fourth place, they were really looped. They invited him in with them and he saw how they spent money, tipping much too high, letting it go like water. Later he told me, 'Jesus, baby, I knew I really fell into something. They couldn't hardly seem to get rid of the geetus fast enough.' Or anyway, something like that."

Unconsciously, when she mimicked her husband's way of talking, an edge of hatred and contempt touched her voice. Maybe under other circumstances it would have been less obvious, but now I was hanging on every word she said.

"A lucky thing happened in that fourth place. Lucky for Orin, anyway. It was a fairly seedy joint in the fifties, and Mickey Sloan almost got into a fight with one of the customers. Orin broke it up, probably saving Sloan from a beating. And Sloan was drunk, but not so drunk he didn't realize what had happened. From that minute on, Orin was his bosom pal. He wouldn't think of taking the train back home, he said. Orin was going to drive them. He offered Orin fifty dollars to do it. Hannah Howard still had enough sense left to know that wasn't so smart. She put up a little fuss, but by the time they got out to the cab, Orin supporting her and Sloan lurching across the sidewalk alongside of them, she had passed out. They dumped her in the back of the cab, where she snored the whole way up to Putnam County, Orin said.

"It was after three in the morning when they got there. Sloan had sobered up a little, but not much. Without help, he wouldn't have been able to get Hannah Howard into the house. Orin, naturally, offered to help. They didn't look like the sort of people who'd have all that money to burn. Even the house was just a run-down clapboard place, one story, and probably mortgaged to the hilt. Since there wasn't any garage, a car was parked out front. Orin even noticed that. It was five years old at least, had a dented fender and needed a paint job. He'd run into something big, he knew that. Just how big it was, though, he was still to find out."

"Okay, okay," I said, "skip the details."

"You didn't believe me, Chuck. I have to convince you I'm telling the truth. We'll be there in a few minutes."

A hoarse voice said: "I believe you now." It was my own voice.

"Well, Orin helped Sloan get the woman inside. It was a run-down, uncared-for place, dirty, cheaply furnished, with paint scabbing off the walls. Orin was more amazed all the time. Where had they got hold of that kind of money? He didn't know, but he was determined to find out."

"Or at least to see if he could latch onto some of that money for himself."

"Yes, that's true. Who wouldn't have? But by then Sloan had sobered enough to want Orin out of there in a hurry. Orin talked him into one for the road. They had two drinks together, the alcohol working on Sloan—but not enough. They were in the kitchen, drinking at the table. Hannah Howard they'd left on the sofa in the living room, still passed out cold. There was a rolling pin on the drain board near the sink and—"

"Why don't you tell me the color of the tablecloth?" I asked sarcastically.

"Well, in a way you're as bad as Orin. The idea of money you were ready to accept, but not that much money. I want you to believe every single thing I'm telling you is the truth. Anyway, Orin got behind Sloan and picked up the rolling pin and hit him with it. Sloan didn't even fall off the chair. His head just slumped forward on the table and he was out colder than Hannah Howard.

"Orin's idea was to take the house apart looking for money, but he hardly had to. He started in back, in their bedroom, finding the luggage right away. It was on the floor in the closet and it looked brand-new. What were they doing with three pieces of brand-new luggage? It didn't make sense, so Orin pulled the gladstone bag out. It was in front. He unbuckled the straps, and opened it, and the way he tells it he went crazy for a minute, crouching there and looking at all that money in tens and twenties and fifties, piled into the gladstone in stacks, stuffed in, squeezed in, making the soft leather bulge there was so much of it. Didn't you notice the bag at the hotel?"

I said I noticed it. I had to clear my throat to get the words out. I could hardly talk.

"So, crazy like that, wild with the idea of all that money, Orin didn't know what to do. It didn't take much figuring to decide the money was hot, though. Still, the bills were small, they didn't run in series, and only a fraction of them were crisp and new," Bunny took a deep breath and let it out through her mouth, fogging the windshield. "Orin began stuffing his pockets. At first it never entered his mind to look into the other two suitcases or maybe just pack up the gladstone and get out of there. He stuffed a few thousand dollars into his pockets, all he could cram in. By the time he finished, bills were scattered all over the floor. He wasn't thinking logically. He was wild, just plain wild. You know, flying off in all directions? He went back to the kitchen and saw Sloan was still passed out. Just then he heard Hannah Howard groaning in the living room. Not wanting to go out front where she might see him, he ran out the back way. There's a closed-in porch behind the kitchen, and Orin went through there. He tripped over something and went sprawling. It was a pile of old magazines, and one of them fell open. Getting up, Orin could see it pretty clearly in the light from the kitchen. It was a confession magazine, the kind Hannah Howard would read, and some of the pages were loose and scattered around the porch. Orin stopped to pick them up. That shows how wild he was, because he hadn't done a thing about all that loose money in the bedroom."

"For crying out loud, will you get to the point?"

"All right. Orin saw that someone had cut words from the loose pages of the confession magazine with a scissors. It hit him like a ton of bricks, because the only thing he could think of, the only reason someone would cut up a magazine like that, was for a ransom note."

"Or blackmail," I suggested.

"Yes, but the papers had been full of the kidnapping story all week. That made things look different to Orin. Hadn't the papers said that the money was in small, unmarked bills? There was a pretty big rumpus about that, maybe you remember. One New York tabloid broke police confidence on the story, and after that there was nothing the cops could do. In a few hours it appeared on every news wire in the country. So, figuring the money couldn't be traced, Orin went back to the bedroom, repacked most of the bills that had fallen on the floor in the gladstone, and took it. He ran with it out front, through the living room. Hannah Howard had vomited, that's why she'd been groaning, but she'd passed out again. Orin ran out to his cab, threw the gladstone in the trunk, locked it and started driving."

Bunny lit a cigarette and took two deep drags on it before she went on talking. "Then he started getting a guilty conscience. Oh, not about the money, but if Sloan and the Howard woman were the kidnappers he'd been reading about, he couldn't just let it drop. At the time, you see, no one knew Teddy Walling was dead, had been dead, in fact, all week. And an anonymous phone call to the police couldn't get Orin into any trouble, so he stopped at an all-night roadhouse and made the call, speaking to a deputy Norstad at the County Sheriff's office.

"After that, Orin drove back to New York. On the way back he decided to let the money cool off for a while, so before pulling into the taxi garage he checked the gladstone bag at the baggage counter in Grand Central and mailed the claim check to himself care of general delivery at the main post office in Queens where we live.

"The next day it was in the papers how the Teddy Walling kidnappers had been apprehended and how they confessed and led the FBI to the boy's body and everything. I remember Orin was nervous and jumpy, but he hadn't told me anything yet. You see, we'd split up once and got back together and were on the verge of another break. We just never got along. Anyway, a couple of days later the FBI sent two agents to talk to

Orin."

"The FBI? How'd they ever tie him up with it?"

"That was easy. They traced back over Sloan and Hannah Howard's trail that night, and someone at that dive in the Fifties remembered how the two of them got in a cab and even remembered which company it belonged to. The police or the FBI checked with Orin's dispatcher, and that was that.

"They were looking for the missing ransom money and though Orin was scared he wouldn't talk. They even got him to admit he'd made the anonymous phone call, but that wasn't the same as taking the money. They served him a subpoena as a witness at the Sloan-Howard trial and he admitted everything all over again except about taking the money. They didn't push it. After all, he was a hero; he'd fingered Sloan and Hannah Howard for the police, hadn't he? And they were the ones the state wanted to send to the electric chair, not Orin.

"Everything went all right until after the trial. By then Orin had told me the whole story. The first thing I made him do was remail the claim check to himself care of general delivery at a different post office. Otherwise, there was the chance it might get lost if it stayed at the main post office without anyone coming to pick it up. So Orin mailed it three more times in the next few weeks.

"Then one day Norstad came to see us. You'll remember he was the deputy sheriff, down in Putnam County, who'd taken Orin's anonymous call. He testified at the trial too, as the arresting officer. Well, he came busting in on us, soft spoken with that deep voice of his but arrogant and sure of himself too, accusing Orin of taking the money and claiming he could prove it. He—"

"Now I get it," I said. "Norstad, he's the big guy who came around to the hotel yesterday, isn't he?"

"I'm almost sure of it. Well, he visited us twice, almost scaring Orin out of his wits. I was pretty scared too, I guess. But I wanted that money—and I still want it. After a while it got so every time someone came to the door we thought it would be the police with a warrant for our arrest. Then, the third time—that was about ten days ago—Norstad laid it on the line for us. He said he'd split the money with us, said that was his price for letting us go free.

"If you remember the newspaper stories, the papers said only the two-suiter, stuffed with ninety thousand dollars of the quarter of a million in ransom money, was recovered. That left the gladstone in the Grand Central baggage room and the third bag, a small duffle. I'm pretty well convinced Norstad took that the night he arrested Sloan and the Howard woman, but I can't prove it. Why he didn't take the bigger bag instead, I don't know. Maybe it was too big to hide easily and he was in a hurry, something like that.

"Anyway, we still weren't having any of it. So Norstad gave us a cock-and-bull story about the money being marked and how he had contacts who could dispose of it out of the country for us for half the take. The way he explained it, they'd buy it for half its face value in cash and our worries would be over. But although we didn't know the exact amount at the time, we had a pretty good idea what it was. Half of half would leave us only about twenty-five thousand and we weren't happy with the idea. It was pretty obvious Norstad had made up that story to scare us and to keep three-quarters of the money for himself if we split. The money isn't marked. I've seen it."

"They have ways of marking it with ultraviolet light

so you couldn't see it."

"I know, but Norstad didn't spring that on us till he'd tried everything else. He was lying, believe me. Well, Chuck, that brings it almost up to date. We told Norstad to go peddle his papers, as Orin put it. But Orin was still scared—more scared than ever, and not of the police. Scared of Norstad. He said we had to leave the country. I tried to argue him out of it, but he wouldn't budge and I didn't know where he'd sent the claim check the last time. He made me come up here, and said he'd meet me. That was something straight out of a melodrama. There wasn't any reason for it, but Orin got this idea and I couldn't budge him off it, either. So here I am, and Orin's at the Mirror Lake Motel with his sprained ankle and a hundred and seventeen thousand dollars, and Norstad followed him."

"Why didn't he just hijack the money on the road if he followed Orin all the way up from New York?"

"I don't know, maybe he thought I had some of it."

That figured, and I said so. We drove in silence for a few minutes. The snow had held us down to a crawl, so it was almost seven o'clock by the time we went through the main street of Lake Placid and up Route 86 toward the Mirror Lake Motel.

The first snow plow was already laboring along the street in town, though the storm, if anything, had increased in intensity. If you took Orin Kemp's gladstone bag, I thought a little wildly, and opened it in front of the huge steel plow, and if there was no wind, a hundred and seventeen thousand dollars in small bills would be plowed into the forming bank of snow. Then doors would open and people would rush out, scurrying over the snow like beetles on a dunghill, fighting, clawing, pushing, digging for the money, picking it up in wet frozen handfuls, deadly serious, enraptured, ready to do violence for their right to go on digging. And, I thought, the crazy vision fading, there's money and money. Ten dollars takes your girl to a modest dinner and a movie afterwards. Twenty dollars buys a family's groceries for a week. Fifty dollars gets you a pair of skis. A hundred dollars is a down payment on a new car. Five hundred takes you to Europe and back by plane. A thousand dollars buys a one-carat diamond in a Tiffany setting. Thirty-five hundred would put a Poma lift on the Whiteface ski slope. Five thousand grubstakes a small business. Twenty thousand dollars would pay off the mortgage on almost any house in Lake Placid. But a hundred and seventeen thousand dollars? It was too much and it made your head swim. You couldn't equate it with anything real, anything specific. You just couldn't swallow the idea of it all at once. It was half of what Sloan and Hannah Howard had killed for and would die for. A man named Walling, whom I'd never met and probably never would, had paid out double it to keep his son alive, and it hadn't been enough. Orin Kemp had it. The deputy, Norstad, wanted it. Bunny wanted it.

And I wanted it.

But there was Bunny. She went with it. She belonged to it. She would fight her husband for it and, I thought, wouldn't stop at anything up to and including murder. In a way, hadn't she killed Jack McCall for it? But, I went on thinking, you took a good long look at it, where did I get off giving Bunny a hard time for what she had done or might do? Hadn't I been guilty, within the bounds of the law, of the same thing with Inez, marrying her and settling down to what quickly had become a third-rate marriage because she owned a million-buck hotel? Don't stand in line, I thought, waiting to see Chuck Odlum pack his two or three hundred bucks worth of worldly possessions to sally forth on his own.

"We're almost there. Aren't you going to say anything?"

"What do you want me to say?"

"I told you everything," Bunny said accusingly. "I thought you loved me."

"You know how I feel about you. What does that have to with it?"

"What does that have to do with it!"

"Sure. We're back where we started from, Bunny. You and Jack McCall."

"Jack McCall is dead."

What was the use? I thought. It wasn't something you could talk about. Talking wouldn't help.

"Aren't you going to help me?"

"Is that what you asked Jack in his cabin?"

"You told me to come out tonight and I came. I helped you."

"Listen," I said, "I didn't kill Jack McCall."

"Oh, so now it comes down to that, does it?"

"I won't lie to you, Bunny. If the money's up for grabs I want it. God knows I want it."

"Don't you think I was taking a chance? Sure, Orin has this bad leg and he can't go anywhere, not yet. And he loves me. He's never stopped loving me. It was the other way around."

"What are you going to do?"

"He's desperate. He has a gun. He sleeps with the gladstone on the bed between him and the wall. I couldn't get it—alone."

"Is it safe for you to go back there?"

"Safe? I don't know. I guess it's safe enough." Bunny's

smile was bitter. "I told him I had to go off by myself and think."

"All night?"

"I got stuck in the snow. What difference does it make if you're not going to help me?"

"I never said I wouldn't."

"You haven't said you would. Help me get the money, Chuck. For us. It could set us up for life. Out West, maybe, someplace like Aspen, Colorado, where there's skiing, if that's what you want. We could buy a place."

"Sure, it sounds great. But we could also spend the rest of our lives running. How far do you think we'd get? And if we did get far enough, what do you think we'd have left for each other?"

"You're scared," she said. "I didn't want to admit it to myself, but you're scared."

Who wouldn't be scared? I thought. But I let that ride, "What about Norstad?"

"You tell me what about him, Chuck."

"I mean, will he try to take the money by force?"

"He hasn't so far. He has this cock-and-bull story about how they marked the money."

"Wait a minute," I said. "He's staying at the Whiteface overnight. If I go back I'll be able to keep an eye on him. I'll know when he leaves."

"You're rationalizing. You want an excuse to drop me off at the motel and go back there. You're scared."

"Look, if I do this I'm going to do it my way. Will you give me until Norstad makes his move?"

Bunny wouldn't look at me. "I can just picture an adding machine or something inside your head, figuring out the debits and credits. I hate it, Chuck. I hate it, thinking of you like that."

"Use your head. I'll be able to keep an eye on Norstad. And anyhow, I couldn't just take off in a pair of fatigues and an old flannel shirt. I'd need some clothes."

"*If* you come back for me."

I pulled the station wagon to a stop about two hundred feet down the road from the Mirror Lake Motel and turned to face her across the front seat, "I'll come back for you," I said,

She slid across the seat and her arms came around my neck. Those eyes swam before my face, pale blue and beautiful, but without any depth. For a second I wondered if maybe the rest of her was like that, fiercely, demandingly beautiful on the outside, but with an emptiness deep inside of her. But that was crazy. I loved her, didn't I? I held her and we kissed. I felt this inarticulate longing just to be with her always well up inside of me. I couldn't speak. Why did the money have to come between us? What did we need it for? Then I thought of Sloan and Hannah Howard living in bitter and frustrated poverty, drinking and dreaming together then finally killing for a six-hour bender on a quarter of a million bucks.

She slipped away from me and opened the door on her side of the car. Her lips formed the words, "I love you," but there wasn't any sound except the wind. I watched her walk away through the snow.

I sat there a while just watching her. She went to the window of their motel unit and looked in, rubbing snow off the pane so she could see. Satisfied, she walked over to their car that was parked in front of the low brick building, and wiped snow off the windshield. She started the car and let the engine warm, then backed it down the driveway through the snow, stopped, put it in low gear and drove up to their unit again. She had been out all night, driving. She'd got stuck in the snow.

She had all the answers, or most of them. She saw me watching her. She didn't wave, but opened the door and went inside and shut it.

I drove away.

CHAPTER TEN

Somewhere in the future there is a world in which Chuck Odlum lives. He's a nice trained seal sort of guy. You know, skis and kind of drifts through life letting his wife run things?

Somewhere in the future there is another world in which Chuck Odlum lives. He's got money and a ski resort out in Aspen, or Squaw Valley, California, or someplace like that, and he's got that woman with the startling blue eyes, the husky eyes. Know him?

And somewhere, another world. A man and a woman in flight, running with a fortune they can't spend keeping them together and making them hate each other and snarl at each other or silently wish each other dead. See him, the shifty-eyed guy with the build of an ex-athlete, drinking himself to an early grave?

Or a world where Jack McCall's body came to the surface somehow after the ice thawed in the spring. The one where the prison guard in the death house passed our love letters back and forth before the execution.

The one where Orin Kemp used his gun on us. The one where Norstad got the money. The one where....

What's the matter with you, I thought, driving back to the Whiteface. Either you want to make a try for Bunny and the money, or you don't. Is that why you stalled her? To have one more look at your life with

Inez before you throw it over for good? You need sleep, brother. You're drunk with the need to sleep. You haven't closed your eyes in twenty-four hours. Is that why you have this cockeyed compulsion to run through all the possibilities? Because it's cockeyed, all right. You can go nuts like that. Ultimately what you would have left would be a man in a straitjacket, babbling, too terrified to move because the slightest motion spawned a new set of possibilities.

I remembered telling Bunny it was more than just a roll in the hay. Well, hadn't it been? And couldn't I prove that now? Not to mention the hundred and seventeen thousand bucks, I told myself as I pulled up in front of the Whiteface.

It was almost seven-thirty on my watch. I went around the side of the building and inside through the kitchen entrance, hoping I wouldn't have to see Inez right away. The clatter of pans and the smell of bacon grilling reminded me how hungry I was, so I went into the kitchen and helped myself to some bacon and eggs. I ate standing up, with the kitchen staff too busy at the bank of stoves and the big work tables to do more than nod at me. I drank a cup of black coffee as hot as I could stand it, wishing I had something to lace it with. Louis, the pastry chef, was mixing batter and throwing his usual morning tantrum. I arbitrated it, hardly knowing what it was about and caring less. All Louis wanted was recognition and pretty soon, though still grumbling, he was satisfied.

I went upstairs and saw one of the cleaning women in the hall.

"Morning, Mr. Odlum."

"Hi. Mrs. Cameron downstairs yet?"

"Yes, sir. A few minutes ago."

Quickly, I went into our room and stripped off the

flannel shirt and fatigue trousers. Putting on a robe, I took them out into the hall and dropped them into the big canvas bag of the cleaning cart. Then I took a shower, first hot, then cold, then hot again. I could feel the streaming water loosening my tense muscles. I was light-headed with fatigue. I dried off, giving myself a brisk towel rubbing, then tied the towel around my waist and opened the bathroom door.

Inez was waiting in the bedroom for me.

She wore a pair of pedal pushers with vertical stripes in three or four different colors accentuating the length of her legs and a red blouse with a froth of white at the throat. Her dark eyes were snapping mad.

"Where did you go last night?"

I hadn't prepared a story. There was no story I could think of which could explain my being out all night in a snowstorm.

"Remind me to let you read my diary," I said.

"Who was she? Who's the girl, Chuck?"

"As a matter of fact, there were three of them," I said. "I have a pretty rough schedule, only three hours to a customer."

"Well, what else can I think?"

"I can't stop you from thinking."

"I'm not going to stand for this, Chuck."

"So?"

She looked at me coldly, as at an insect impaled on a pin. "I'm not going to stand for this. I want you to know that."

I didn't say anything.

"You're deliberately goading me."

"Look who's talking."

"I asked you, what else can I think?"

All I had left, and it wasn't much, was a change of pace. I went over to her and grabbed her arms above the elbows, bringing my face dose to hers and staring into her angry eyes. "Mrs. Cameron, ma'am, wouldn't I be kind of crazy to play the field if I have you?"

"I—I want to believe you, Chuck. But I don't want you to lie to me."

"Shh," I said, kissing her lightly on the lips. "You wouldn't want a growing boy to miss out on his sleep." I went over to the bed and sat down on the edge. I slipped under the covers and sat there looking at her.

Her eyes softened. "That's it. You're just like a little boy."

So she came over and tucked me in, giving me the full motherly treatment including the goodnight kiss. The scent of her perfume and the light touch of her long dark hair on my face brought a stirring of remembered desire, but then she was standing at the door and watching me uncertainly and then she blew me another goodnight kiss and the door shut behind her and I was alone.

I must have fallen asleep right away. I don't even remember an interval of thinking, of drifting off. I slept like a dead man, without regrets, without dreams, without plans.

The jangling of the bedside telephone jarred me out of sleep. I fumbled on the night table for the phone, knocked it to the floor and picked it up.

"Yeah?"

"I have an outside call for you, Mr. Odlum," the hotel operator said. For a second I heard an open line, then a click.

"Chuck?" I recognized her voice right away. I hoped she hadn't given her name to the operator, then remembered the operator had merely said an outside call.

"Yes, go ahead."

"He's gone, Chuck."

There was a silence. "Yes, go on. I'm listening."

"He took it."

"I'll be right over."

"Hurry. Please hurry."

It didn't really sock me until after I hung up. He was gone, and he'd taken the money. That was when I knew, truly and for the first time, how much I wanted it.

I got out of bed, found a pack of butts on the night table and lit one. I looked at my watch. It was a quarter to nine. I'd been asleep less than an hour. Working fast, I put on ski pants, boots, a turtle-neck sweater and one of those slipover ski jackets with drawstrings. There was a little bourbon left in the night table bottle, and I killed it. I went to the window. You could barely see across the road through the snow.

Hurrying downstairs, I almost made it to the front entrance when Kirby Rowe called me. I could pretend I hadn't heard him, but decided against that. It was something that might be remembered later, if we did anything about Orin Kemp and the money. I had to appear calm but I could feel the tension coiling inside me like an overwound spring.

"What's up, Kirby?"

He fingered his moustache and frowned. "You going down to Placid?"

"Why?"

"Because you'd better do some public relations with the sheriff's substation over there. We've already had one call this morning about McCall's dogs."

"Oh? Who from?"

"Deputy sheriff. A couple of the dogs were spotted outside Keene. One of them attacked a boy right on the main street of Lake Placid."

"Attacked him? They're gentle. They're tame."

"Ordinarily," Kirby Rowe said. "I called the vet in Lake Placid and checked with him. As he sees it, they've been domesticated all their lives and on the loose they don't know how to forage for themselves. They're meat eaters, Chuck. And they've got wolf in their blood."

"You mean they might be dangerous?"

"More so all the time. The deputy said he might have to ask for volunteers to round them up before they really went wild."

"Hell," I said, "they're probably scattered all over the country by now."

"I know. That's what I told him. But I still think you ought to have a look in at his office. He's ripping mad."

"All right." I thought of Bunny and the money. I wanted to get out of there.

"Try to get us off the hook if you can."

"It wasn't our fault. If Jack just—"

"That's not the way he sees it. They're our dogs, he said, so we're responsible."

"Okay, I'll let you know."

I thought he was finished, but he walked in front of me, barring the door, and said, "If the deputy's really serious about a posse, you might pass the vet's advice along to him. The vet says there are two places they're most likely to turn up sooner or later. Back here at their kennels and wherever Jack cut them loose."

I was hardly listening. When I nodded, he stepped aside to let me pass. I opened the door and went out into the snow. The cold hit me in the face like a fist, taking my breath away. By the time I reached the Willys wagon, I felt an odd sensation of thickening in my nostrils. Sometimes in winter you get that around here, for if it's cold enough the moisture in your nostrils will freeze. That meant, in the hour and a half I'd been inside, the thermometer had dropped way below zero. A gust of icy wind flattened me against the door of the station wagon, and I had to fight it to get the door open.

Seconds later I was heading down Route 86, much too fast in the snow, toward Mirror Lake. All I could think of was a hundred and seventeen thousand dollars.

CHAPTER ELEVEN

When I pulled into the motel driveway, their car was gone. I could still see its tire tracks in the snow, though, and at the rate it was falling that meant he hadn't been gone very long.

I jumped out of the Willys, ran through the snow to the door of their unit and pounded on it. Bunny opened it right away, let me inside and leaned against the door to shut it. She stood there with her palms flat against the wood, looking at me. "Thank God you're here."

"Jesus," I said, "did he do that to you?"

There was a blue bruise, roughly oblong and almost the size of a pack of cigarettes, on her cheek.

She nodded slowly. "He knew I'd been out. He was sleeping when I got back, but he knew I'd been out. He was crazy when he got up. He wouldn't listen to anything I said. He had this wild idea I'd seen Norstad, even though he doesn't know Norstad's up here."

"When?" I said.

"He left less than half an hour ago, right before I called you. I couldn't stop him. I tried. He hit me. He could hardly walk, especially with the suitcase. He stumbled out to the car with it and I ran out there, pleading for him to stop. He almost ran me down with the car. Chuck, he's got it. He's got the money. What are we going to do?"

"Take it easy," I said. "Getting hysterical won't help. I've got to think."

"Every minute we stand here talking he's further away."

"You said he wanted to go up into Canada?"

"Yes. Montreal. It's a big city, he told me. He must have told me a hundred times how we were going to lose ourselves in it, money and all."

"Okay. If he was sold on the idea, there's no reason why he'd change it now. Grab your lumberjacket and let's go after him."

"Yes there is. Don't you see? He knows I know. And he thinks I'm with Norstad. He wouldn't go there now."

I thought a moment. "That's not the way I see it. Sure he knows you know. Wouldn't he figure you'd think just what you told me? That he'd change his plans? If that's the case, why should he? Unless you think he'd drive back down to New York."

She shook her head at once. "No, he's all through with New York. That's where the trial was. That's where the FBI questioned him. He doesn't want any part of it."

She put on her lumberjacket and we went outside, running through the wind and the snow to the station wagon. I started the motor and said: "Look at it this way. Even if he decides Montreal is out, that still leaves the rest of Canada. But the only way you'd have a chance of getting up there through a deep snow like this is using the main road. That's Route 9 out of Plattsburg and straight through to Montreal. So even if he wanted to head for Toronto or someplace else, he'd have to go up that way."

I started driving. She didn't say anything. When we reached the first steep switchback between Mirror Lake and Wilmington I had to pump the brake pedal until we reduced our speed to fifteen miles an hour despite the four-wheel-drive. Through the wind-driven snow you could hardly see the pines and stands of white birch that flanked the climbing, twisting road.

"We'll never catch him," she said. "Not in this snow with the head start he's got."

I started to say something about four-wheel-drive, but then she suddenly shouted my name. "Chuck! Maybe you saw me. I started the car up before I went in this morning. The gas gauge, Chuck. It was empty. Empty."

"That usually means you have a couple of gallons left."

"Yes, but if he doesn't notice. He was frantic. Norstad does that to him. The only thing he can think of is Norstad."

I drove on without answering her, thinking that was too much to hope for. We passed a sand truck laboring along with a man in a parka standing in the open back, shoveling sand out on the steep curves. Except for that truck, the road was deserted. We drove through Wilmington toward Jay. Here, before dropping down toward the Ausable River and Plattsburg on Lake Champlain, the road reached its highest point. We took another switchback and came out of it on a steep incline, and all at once we drove into a cloud. The world became gray and featureless. It was almost like driving blindfolded. I cut our speed and took the curves as they came, braking for them and gunning the motor slightly to pick up traction just as we hit them. Time and space stretched out in front of us, taut and waiting, like the tension building inside me, and I had to fight myself to keep from going dangerously fast. After all, I told myself, he came this way, didn't he? He had to go through it too. But he was desperate. Well, wasn't I desperate too?

Then suddenly we began picking up speed as the road dropped out of the highest hills. The station wagon lurched when I put it in low gear. I saw brightness up ahead. Seconds later the cloud was above and behind us and we were driving through the white, endless snow.

In a little while we passed a sign which said, *ESSO, 1000 yards on the left, last gas for five miles.* I didn't think anything of it at first, but then Bunny cried:

"Chuck! Chuck, look!"

I saw it right after she did, a car parked about a hundred yards beyond the Esso sign on the snow-covered shoulder of the road alongside a stand of white birch. It was their car.

I pulled up behind it and we got out running. I reached it before she did. Orin Kemp wasn't in it. I tried the door handle, but it was locked. I looked in the window and saw the gladstone bag on the floor in the rear.

"We've got to break in," I said wildly. "He must have run out of gas like you said. He's probably getting it at the station up ahead." I pounded at the door and tugged impotently at the handle.

Bunny was smiling and yanking at my shoulder, trying to pull me out of the way. "I have a key, silly," she said. "Move over." I saw the key in her hand. I saw those blue eyes, bright as glass, glittering. Coolly, she inserted the key in the lock. Then the smile dropped off her face.

"I can't turn it," she said.

"Let me."

I tried to twist the key. It wouldn't budge. "You sure it's the right key?" I demanded. I was shouting.

"Of course I'm sure."

I tried again. No dice. A hundred and seventeen thousand bucks, and we couldn't open the door.

Calm down, I told myself. Calm down, damn you. My hands were shaking. Then I laughed. It was almost a sob. Wasn't it cold enough for the lock to have frozen in a few minutes?

I took the key out and gave it to Bunny. We huddled over it alongside the car, trying to block the fierce wind. I fumbled in my pocket for matches and lit one. The wind blew it out instantly. I lit another. I dropped the book of matches.

"Get a grip on yourself," Bunny said. "Here."

Unzipping her lumberjacket, she held the key inside it to shield it from the wind. I struck another match and applied the flame to the key. This time it didn't go out. I held it there until I burned my fingers. Then I grabbed the key from Bunny and jammed it into the lock. It turned without any trouble. I swung the door open.

The first bullet *zinged* through air a few inches from my head before I heard the flat, cracking sound of the shot.

"Get down!" I hollered instinctively, and Bunny squatted.

The second shot went wild. But I saw him hobbling along the road. He was still about sixty or seventy yards away, struggling through the snow with a big gasoline can in one hand and the gun in the other.

"I'll get you, Norstad!" he screamed. "I'll get you!"

He fired again and collapsed to one knee as his bad

leg gave under him. I thought fast. If we stayed where we were, we were sitting ducks. If we made a run back to the station wagon, we were also sitting ducks, even if we got inside. If we ran around behind the car, that would only delay it. He'd still come for us, and he'd get us.

When he climbed to his feet and began limping toward us again, I saw the birches. They grew down the flank of a hill almost to the edge of the road. Our one chance would be in there.

I took Bunny's hand and ran with her behind the car. He'd held his fire after getting up, but then the gun roared. We crouched behind the car.

"I'm scared," Bunny said. "Now I'm scared, Chuck. He'll kill us. He'll kill us."

The worst part of it was not hearing his footsteps on the snow. But the longer we waited the better chance he'd have of hitting us when we made our break.

Still holding Bunny's hand, I broke away from the car and ran in a zig-zagging crouch toward the woods. Bunny cried out and ran with me. Kemp fired once, and then we were in among the trees and plunging uphill through the deep snow.

Floundering, stumbling, we kept going. The hill climbed steeply to a ridge. I couldn't see beyond it, but this was wild, desolate country with another ridge on the far side of Route 86 so that the road twisted and turned, riverlike, through a narrow defile. If we made the ridge, I thought, we'd be safe. He couldn't hope to keep up with us with his bad leg. But then I thought he might get smart and go back to the station wagon and yank out the distributor cap or something. Except for the gas station up ahead, we'd be in serious trouble, for you could freeze to death in a short time in the numbing cold. And at the very least that would give him back his head start.

We couldn't make the ridge directly, for the slope became too steep. We had to parallel it for several hundred yards through the trees, angling away from the road. I looked back once and couldn't see Kemp. He'd be following our footsteps, though. I couldn't see the road either. We were now about two hundred yards from it, I figured, and angling further up the wooded slope with every step we took.

Finally I found a cut where the slope leveled off. It might have been a frozen stream bed, snow covered. I climbed through it to the ridge and pulled Bunny after me. She wanted to keep going, but I yanked her down beside me. I wanted to see what Kemp would do.

Peering over the ridge and screened by a clump of white birch, I let my eyes follow our trail through the trees. At first I didn't see him, but I could hear him pushing through the brittle, frozen undergrowth that hadn't been covered by the snow.

After about five minutes, I saw him. He'd left the gas can on the road. He came limping up slowly, the gun in his hand. Once he stopped and looked up, staring straight at me but unable to see me. He had to take off his glasses and wipe the snow off them on his sleeve. He was panting, the gusts of vapor coming from his slack mouth. And he was close enough so that I could see he was in pain.

Bunny tugged at my sleeve, but I shook her off. I had to know if he'd return to the cars. We couldn't just keep running if there was no reason to run.

Kemp put his glasses back on, then snarled in disgust, took them off and jammed them in the pocket of his trench coat. Rage twisted his face as he struggled up the hill again. He came plodding up, dragging his injured leg, squinting myopically into the snow.

He wasn't more than fifty feet from us when he caught his foot on something, probably an exposed root hidden under the snow, and fell. He howled and rolled over, dropping the gun. He sat up covered with snow, squinting, facing us. Then he to get to his feet. He howled again, like an animal in a trap, and collapsed. His shoulders jerking with the effort, he began to drag himself toward the gun.

You didn't have to be a genius to know he'd hurt the other leg.

For a while, fascinated, I watched him. His legs were useless. He had to drag himself forward, his elbows bent, like a soldier pinned down by enemy fire. Pretty soon he straightened his arms out, groping for handholds in the undergrowth. He'd grab a bush and the brittle branches would snap off. He was making almost no headway. He hadn't cut the distance between him and the gun in half, and that was only seven or eight yards, when this idea hit me full grown. I didn't have to think it out. It was there, and it was perfect.

I got up and went down the hill to him. I picked up the gun before his groping fingers could touch it. He looked up at me. Falling, he'd lost his hat. His red face and thin hair were covered with snow. He spat out of his mouth and cursed me. He never even saw me. All the time he thought I was Norstad.

Bunny came running down the hill, grabbing the slender boles of the birches to check her momentum. She stared down at her husband and didn't say a word. She looked up at me while I pocketed the gun. Her eyes were narrow slits against the wind and the snow, but her lips were moist and parted as if she'd just been made love to. I knew somehow she had this idea too. Her eyes opened wider and looked the question at me. I nodded. I was all caught up in it. The best thing that could have happened had happened. I didn't want to think of anything else, but I saw the ugly bruise on Bunny's face and if I'd had any doubts, that made up my mind.

We went down the hill slowly, not wanting to fall as he had fallen. It was harder going down than it had been climbing up. For maybe half the distance we could hear his cursing. There seemed to be no end to it, but then, all at once, it was taken up by the wind and we didn't hear it any longer. Once I turned around to look back. He had moved very little if at all. He was a small dark figure sprawled there on the snow in the numbing, killing cold. One leg sprained and the other one maybe broken.

We reached the car. The door was the way we had left it, open. I reached in over the front seat, lifted the rear door lock button and waited. Bunny opened the rear door. I got the gladstone bag out and carried it to the station wagon.

I put it inside and we climbed in. Then I remembered the gas can and went out in the snow looking for it. He had set it down near the fender on the other side of the car. I didn't touch it.

I got back into the station wagon, started the motor and sawed the wagon back and forth across the road until I could turn it. Then I started to drive back toward Mirror Lake.

That was when I looked at Bunny. She sat slumped down and had covered her face with her hands. She made a stifled noise. I couldn't tell if she was trying not to laugh or trying not to cry.

CHAPTER TWELVE

Neither one of us spoke until we passed through Wilmington. The blizzard howled through the timber on either side of the road and had piled snow in great drifts higher than the roof of the station wagon on the town's single business street. Finally I said:

"With a little luck, nobody's going to pass your car until we get back."

"Oh, are we going back?"

"Sure. And if somebody drives by, they'll probably see the gas station sign and figure he's walked up ahead for gas. The only thing I don't like, they might start worrying about their gas can in the station."

"What are we going back for, Chuck? Do we have to?"

"We have to. We've got to pack your luggage at the Mirror Lake Motel and bring it back to the car. Then, after that, I find you. You're concerned because your husband hasn't returned. We drive to the gas station looking for him, just as confused as they'll be. By the time anybody finds him ..."

"Chuck, how long will it take my husband to die?"

"Don't talk like that," I said harshly. "Don't even think like that. From now on you've got to play a role and you've got to make it good. The state police will question you. They won't be able to figure out why he went off into the timber, and neither will you. It's a mystery they'll never solve. By the time they find him, the wind and snow will have covered our footprints. Don't you see, it's perfect."

She lit a cigarette. Her hands were steady, but I didn't like the way she was sitting there, staring straight ahead as if hypnotized. Maybe she was seeing her husband trying to crawl through the snow.

"Did anybody at the motel see him leave alone?"

"No-o. I'm almost sure."

"Good. I'll go in there with you. I'll limp back to the car after we pack. In this storm if anyone sees me they'll think I'm Kemp. Then you pay the bill, we drive back there and—"

"You already told me."

"All right. After that we'll have to keep away from each other. I don't know how long. We can meet somewhere later. I'll have to take the money, because of Norstad. He might come looking for you."

"Yes," she said after a while. I could tell she wasn't in love with that part of it, but she knew I was right. "I hadn't thought of that."

We drove another mile or so in silence. "How do you feel?"

"Empty. I could use a stiff drink. Just all empty inside, Chuck."

"I know. I know how it is."

"No, you don't. How could you? I lived with him for four years. I ate with him. I talked with him. I shared his secrets. I slept with him. Oh, I guess I stopped loving him a long time ago. He was cruel and shallow. He wasn't very smart. We fought a lot. I told you, didn't I, that I left him once? But I came back and that must have meant something. And he—he never stopped loving me. Despite everything, even knowing how I felt, I think, he never stopped wanting me. And now … I killed him."

I watched the road and didn't say anything.

"Well, it's the same as killing him, isn't it? It's murder?"

"It's not murder if nobody figures it for murder."

"That's easy for you to say."

"Listen, I—"

"I'm sorry, Chuck. We're in this together." Then she threw a curve. Her mind worked so fast, I couldn't keep up with her. She asked: "What if he doesn't die?"

"Don't talk like that. How can he survive?"

"But what if he does?" She lit another cigarette. "What if they find him before we come back?"

"The odds are a thousand to one against it in this storm. We haven't passed a car all morning. Don't worry about it."

"Chuck, we're going to enjoy that money."

"I know. I know we are, baby."

"We're going to do everything we both ever wanted."

"Yes."

Just before noon we approached the driveway of the Mirror Lake Motel. I started to swing in but at the last minute kept going straight. I'd seen a car parked in front of the office. A man was just getting out, a big fellow with a tweed overcoat.

"Oh God!" Bunny cried. "It's Norstad."

As we passed, he went into the office.

"God," Bunny said again.

"All right. All right, take it easy. We'll just have to wait, that's all." But I could feel it too, gnawing away inside of me. Norstad would know, if he searched their room, they'd gone without their luggage. Would they let him search it? Sure they would, I thought. He had his buzzer, didn't he? He was a cop. Still, we needed that luggage. We had no kind of story at all without it. What would they be doing driving in this storm unless they had packed and pulled out for good?

We drove a little ways. Bunny sat twisting her hands in her lap. "I'll go crazy if I don't have something to drink," she said. "This waiting will drive me crazy."

"We can't be seen together. You know that."

"The lodge? Isn't there more rum there?"

Why not? I thought. Figure it would take Norstad half an hour talking in the office, conning them into letting him search the Kemp's room and then actually searching it. We couldn't chance coming back for at least an hour, and in this weather there wouldn't be anyone at the lodge. We could hole up there as well as anywhere else, and now that she'd mentioned it the idea of a drink appealed to me too, for there was still plenty we had to do and it might help unjangle our nerves.

"I've got one stop to make first," I said. "Okay?"

"Yes, whatever you say."

We drove the mile or so into Lake Placid and I parked off the main street alongside the sheriff's substation. Dropping in there would give me a reason for being out. The street was deserted, so I knew she'd be all right in the station wagon. I squeezed her hand and felt her return the pressure. Then I got out and ran around the corner through the snow to the front of the substation. It was a one-story red-brick building with an office in front and the lockup in the rear.

I opened the door, stamped the snow off my boots on the mat and saw Deputy Joe Moon sitting with his feet up on his desk behind the railing that divided the room. It was warm in there. A potbellied stove glowed cherry-red in the middle of the floor.

"Shut it before we freeze to death," Joe Moon said in his booming voice. He was a roly-poly man of about forty or forty-five with a pink complexion, two chins too many, warm blue eyes with laughter wrinkles at their corners and corn silk hair combed carefully over his bald spot.

I shut the door against the wind and he said, "Oh,

it's you. Boy, you sure have been giving me a hard time." He swung his feet down and stared at me, then the round face broke into a rueful grin. "Hell's bells, Chuck, we already had eight-nine calls this morning. They've seen those dogs of yours just about everywhere, and we have to check all the stories out. The boys just love it, sloshing through the snow." Then the grin left his face. "We did have a little fellow got himself bit in Lake Placid, though."

"I know, Joe. I heard. He all right?"

"Yeah, they scared the dog off. Left teeth marks on his arm is about the size of it. But it could have been worse. Lots worse. Say," he added, "those dogs wouldn't be rabid, would they now?"

"Not a chance. They got their shots."

"What you aiming to do?"

"That's what I came to see you about."

"McCall ain't back yet?"

I shook my head.

"The no-good bastard, what the hell's the matter with him?"

I shrugged and said, "Kirby Rowe told me something about a posse. I'll give you half a dozen volunteers from the Whiteface staff any time you say."

He grinned again. "Yeah, volunteers. They're gonna love you."

Then I remembered there was something Kirby Rowe wanted me to tell him, but I couldn't recall what it was, for I'd hardly been listening to Kirby.

Joe Moon got up, opened the fire door of the potbellied stove and shoveled some coal in. "Well, I guess that's all any of us can do," he said. "No sense getting a posse started till she stops blowing outside, though. Man, what a storm! The old lady wanted to settle in Florida too. That's all I hear these days."

"Let me know when you need our people."

"Right, Chuck. I'll give you a call. And do me a favor, will you? Don't go importing any polar bears into the county come next winter."

"Cross my heart," I said. We both grinned and I went back outside. Joe Moon was putting his feet back up on the desk when I left.

I climbed into the station wagon. Bunny said, "I missed you. Just five minutes, and I missed you. I'm like a schoolgirl with you."

"We'll have the rest of our lives together."

"I know. I can get all weak inside just thinking of it."

Then, as we started to drive, I foolishly said, "It sure is cold out there."

Bunny opened her mouth to say something, but averted her head and was silent. Me and my big yap, I thought. That got her started on Kemp all over again. But what else could we have done? Kemp wouldn't have given up the money without a fight, and even if we got it he'd have known we had it and that would have meant running. Besides, it wasn't the same as murdering him in cold blood, was it? Like hell it wasn't, I thought. You show me just one difference, brother. Just one single difference.

"I love you, Bunny."

"... I love you too."

Justification by rote phrase, I thought. But how much would it mean if we couldn't blot out the memory of what we'd done? I didn't say anything else until we reached the lodge.

A high drift had piled up around the outside ski rack, but the door was clear. I opened it and we went inside, stamping our feet. It was cold enough in there to see the exhalation of our breath, but at least there wasn't any wind. While Bunny waited at the counter

I found an unopened bottle of rum and broke the seal with my thumb nail.

"To the future together," I said, handing the pint bottle to Bunny. She tipped it up solemnly and drank. I had to pry it out of her hand. "Whoa," I said. "You're going to need a clear head for the rest of it."

"I don't want to think about it."

"Okay, one more. Just a small one."

I gave her back the bottle and she tilted it again. She passed it to me, her eyes watering, and I took a single long pull, feeling the rum hit bottom and spread out warmly almost at once.

"You're very beautiful," I said. She was too. "You know it?"

"I like to hear you say it."

I kissed her lightly on the lips and she clung to me for a moment. Outside, the wind shrieked through the pine branches.

"We've got to get a move on," I said.

She let go and drew away. "I'm as ready as I'll ever be."

"Come on."

At the door I paused. "You want the rum for later?"

"Yes, please. I'll wait in the car."

She went outside and I walked back to the counter for the pint of rum. I screwed the cover on tight and slipped it in the zipper pocket of my ski jacket. Just as I turned around, Bunny screamed.

I ran across the floor of the lodge and outside. I stood there for an instant in the wind and the snow, my mind a complete blank, not knowing what to expect. She screamed again, in terror, and then I saw her.

She was down on the snow halfway to the station wagon, desperately trying to twist away from the gray-coated husky that had pinned her down with its forepaws. I saw the big muscular body, that had chow and malamute and wolf in it, move, saw the head go down. Then the husky's yelp and Bunny's scream rose together in the wind and I had Orin Kemp's gun in my hand. They rolled over together in a flurry of snow, the husky yelping. Even as I ran I knew I couldn't shoot to hit the husky. It was on top of her, the paws bent and the body down almost flat. I got as close as I could and fired into the air. The husky howled and jerked its head up. I'll never forget that. I saw those eyes like glass, pale blue and depthless, in the husky's head. Bunny's eyes. And there was blood, her blood, on its muzzle.

I went wild then. I yelled and fired again, but the gun was empty. I threw it and struck the husky just back of the shoulder. It jerked up and away from Bunny, looking at me, undecided as to whether it should attack or flee. I kicked it with the hard heavy toe of my ski boot with all my weight behind it. The husky's head snapped back and it yelped in pain. I lashed out again with my foot and felt the solid contact even through the ski boot. Two kicks like that, with a ski boot that weighed three pounds and was as hard and unyielding as wood, might have killed a man, but the husky only floundered in the snow, its flanks heaving. It got up, the splotchy tongue hanging out, and glared at me,

"Can you get up?" I asked Bunny. I couldn't look at her; I couldn't take my eyes off the dog.

She made a sound that might have been affirmative. "Keep behind me and get into the car. Slowly. Don't run."

I didn't hear her moving in the snow. I couldn't see her. I watched the husky, that was still panting and watching me. After a long time I heard the station wagon door open and shut.

"Chuck...." Her voice was faint and seemed far away.

I backed slowly toward where I thought the gun had fallen in the snow. I bent and groped for it while the husky took a step toward me, slowly. Then my hand closed on cold metal and I straightened up and edged toward the station wagon. Once I stumbled and almost fell. If I did, I thought the husky would jump me. I kept going, one slow sideways edging step at a time until I hit the fender of the Willys wagon. Bunny had leaned across the seat to open the door. Slipping in, I pulled it shut. The big gray dog, wild with hunger, stood its ground, watching us. When we swung around and drove away, it still hadn't moved.

Until then I didn't look at Bunny. Now, when I did, I cried out. The skin and flesh had been torn from her cheekbone in a triangular flap that hung loose almost down to her jaw. There were tooth marks on either side of it. Her eyes were glazed and the blood had soaked into the collar of her lumberjacket.

I brought the station wagon to a lurching stop and gave her the rum. Her hands were trembling so much she couldn't hold it, so I held the bottle to her lips and she drank. I squeezed her shoulder. It was shaking uncontrollably.

"Chuck, wh-what are we going to do?"

"I'll have to get you to a doctor."

"You can't. Not now."

"I've got to."

She shuddered. "Give me your handkerchief."

She pressed it, folded, against her cheek to stem the bleeding.

"Listen," she said. "You've got to listen."

"I've got to get you to a doctor."

"And ruin everything? It can wait. Listen. You go

into the motel. Pack our things. Just two bags. Leave the money on the dresser. All right? All right, Chuck?"

I nodded slowly. She was right of course. If we didn't go ahead with our plans, everything was ruined. But looking at her, sitting there like that with the terrible wound on her beautiful face, I couldn't think.

"Then we'll go back there, where we left the car. He ... went for gas. When he didn't come back, I got worried and ... went looking for him. The dog ... attacked me there. You found me, drove it off. Maybe ... maybe the dog chased me into the woods. Maybe Orin went after us up there and the dog ran away and I wandered back to the road, dazed." She made that sound again, that I couldn't tell if it was laughing or crying. "And Orin hurt his leg and ... You thought it was perfect before? It's perfect ... now. But hurry up. Just hurry up."

I kissed her, alongside of where she held the handkerchief. Her skin was like ice.

Then I started to drive, thinking that she was right, that now it really was perfect, and hating myself for it.

CHAPTER THIRTEEN

Norstad's car was gone when we returned to the Mirror Lake Motel. I parked in front of the last unit in the low brick building. There were two other cars in the driveway: one, snowed in, must have belonged to the owner and the other was in front of the small restaurant.

"Hurry," Bunny said in toneless urgency.

She gave me the key and I went in there. Right away I knew Norstad had been through the small, cheaply furnished room, for he hadn't bothered to hide the thorough search he'd made. The beds had been pulled away from the walls, a trap door in the ceiling which must have led to a storage attic was out of line and the clothes hanging in the closet had been slid and bunched at one end of the hanger rod. I got up on the chair which Norstad had left under the trap door and straightened it, wondering as I did so what Norstad had told the motel proprietor.

Then I pulled the two suitcases from the closet floor and began to stuff clothing into them. I thought of Bunny waiting out there in pain. I thought of Kemp, dead or dying up in the mountains. I wanted to hurry for Bunny, but knew I had to give Kemp enough time to die. How long would it take? I didn't know, but unable to use his legs he'd hardly be able to move at all and that, more than anything, would kill him swiftly in the subzero cold. After I'd removed their belongings from the closet, the dresser and the medicine chest in the bathroom, I deliberately sat down on the edge of one of the beds and smoked a cigarette. A few more minutes, I thought, knowing I'd hurry once I saw Bunny again. He'd hardly been out there two hours yet. Was he already dead? No, probably not. But now long would it take him to die, four hours? Five? Most of the day maybe? Simmer down, I told myself, you don't have to find him right away.

I finished the cigarette and brought the two suitcases out to the station wagon.

"Did you pay?" Bunny asked.

"No. I forgot."

"Leave it on the dresser with the key. Fourteen dollars."

I had to ask Bunny for the money because I didn't

have any with me. She was carrying a red leather wallet in the pocket of her ski pants. When she handed it to me I saw there were just two bills in it, a ten and a five.

"That cleans you out," I said.

"Yes." She tried to smile. "All I have left is half of a hundred and seventeen thousand dollars."

I went back inside with the money and left it on the dresser with the key. Just as I returned to the station wagon, a man and a woman came out of the restaurant and ran laughing through the snow to the car parked outside. I didn't like that, but they probably wouldn't notice us and if they did it wouldn't mean anything to them later.

I got behind the wheel of the station wagon and started to drive. Two hours now, right on the button. He was still alive. He almost had to be still alive.

"When I find you," I told Bunny, "you're going to be like in a state of shock. You won't be able to talk coherently. You won't say anything about your husband. Or maybe you can put on a hysterical crying act if you want. All right?"

"Stop worrying. I know what I have to do."

We drove back through Wilmington, not talking. I felt the tension mount in me, gripping my stomach like a clenching fist, squeezing it into a tight jumpy knot. The next few hours would tell. Everything depended on the next few hours.

"Could I have another drink?"

"Sure, but go easy. If you were in shock I wouldn't give you alcohol."

"You're not a doctor. What's the difference?"

"I run a ski school. It's one of the things you're supposed to know."

"Just a little one, please." When I nodded, she took

the bottle that was on the seat between us and drank. I wiped condensed moisture off the windshield as we started climbing into the high hills. The snow and the wind and the urgency knotting my insides threw my time sense for a loop. It seemed to take forever to reach their car.

"Does it hurt bad?"

"I can stand it. But I wish you'd shut off the heater. The cold numbs it."

I turned off the heater and kept driving. "He have anything to eat this morning?"

"Not unless he grabbed a bite after he left. I ate in the restaurant while I was waiting for you, but he just ran out to the car and drove off. Must we talk?"

Nothing to eat since last night, I thought, meant no fuel to supply the heat his body would need to stay alive. It was better all the time. Within a few moments of turning the heater off it had become fiercely cold in the station wagon. My fingers, even inside the ski mittens, were painfully stiff. But I like the cold, and it was nothing to what Kemp had to face.

Suddenly we went down a hill and slipped around a curve and came upon the Esso sign. I saw their car, then, just up the road. I parked behind it again and got out. Our footprints leading off into the timber had been covered. I looked up the hill at the birches. I shuddered. It was as if we had gone back in time and arrived the first time and had just left Kemp out there, high among the birches, to die. Leave us not get morbid about it, I thought. What's the matter with you? You had to do it, and you did. But if I felt this way now, I wondered what it would be like later.

I went back to the car and opened the door on Bunny's side. "You'll have to get out," I said gently. "I'm going to find you now. In case things happen fast, we'll want footprints."

She got out obediently, still holding the handkerchief against her face. I made her walk a little ways up the hill in weaving circles, then I told her to sit down in the snow. I walked directly to her, got one arm under her thighs and one under her shoulders and lifted her.

Just then, I heard a car coming from the direction of Wilmington. I felt Bunny stiffen in my arms, but I kept walking. "That's all right," I said. "I found you. I just now found you."

The car came around the curve and stopped behind the station wagon. I could feel my heart start to hammer; it was the car that had been parked outside the restaurant at the Mirror Lake Hotel. All right, all right, I thought, so what? They stopped there for lunch. They're driving through to Montreal. They wouldn't have noticed you there.

The man got out and came running around their car. He was a young fellow, not over twenty-five, wearing a black nylon zipper jacket and a bright red ski cap. "What's the trouble?" he hailed me. "Anything I can do to help?"

"Found her out here," I said, panting. "It looks like she's been bitten."

He helped me get her in the front seat of the station wagon. Would he notice their suitcases in back, and would he remember them? But there were three bags in the wagon, including the gladstone, and I only had to put two in Kemp's trunk. Still, with this fellow around, I wouldn't get the chance to do it.

The window of their car rolled down and a girl's voice called: "What's the matter, Les?"

"He says she's been bitten." Les shouted.

"Bitten?"

Bunny moaned and slid across the front seat, stretching out.

"Can we get her to a doctor?" Les asked me.

"Gas station up ahead. I'll call the state police from there. I'll take care of it."

"Sure we can't help?"

"Say, remember what we heard on the radio?" the girl said. "About those dogs that got loose? Eskimo dogs? I'll bet it was one of them." The wind shrieked. "Listen, did you hear that?"

"It was just the wind," Les said.

"I heard a dog howling. I know when I hear a dog howling, Lester."

"Maybe she's right," I said. They were almost too good to be true. Give the girl a little more time and she might even see a husky fleeing through the timber. I almost wished they'd come along with me to the gas station, but there was still the problem of the two suitcases.

I sat down behind the wheel. Les got in from the other side and helped Bunny into a sitting position. "I'll ride with you," he said, then shouted: "Helen, you follow us."

Les shut the door. Through the rearview mirror I could just see the tan top and handle of one of their suitcases. I started to drive.

"There now, take it easy," Les told Bunny. "It's going to be all right. We're going to take care of you." On cue Bunny whimpered.

It took us only a minute to reach the gas station. I left Les there with Bunny and ran past the pumps to the office. The big plate glass window was coated over with moisture and a light glowed cheerfully through it. I went inside and saw a wizened old man in knee boots, corduroy pants and an open mackinaw sitting on a chair tilted back against the wall and reading a true crime magazine, his thin lips moving as he spelled out the words.

"In a jiffy," he mumbled, and his lips went to work again.

"Listen," I said. "Call the state police. I have a girl out in the car that's been hurt."

He didn't look up. "Your girl?"

"No. I found her down the road."

"Beat up on?" He looked up at me. His eyes were small and deep set and still more concerned with the tales of horror they'd been reading than with what I'd told him. "Young feller," he said, "let me tell you a thing or two about finding bodies. Twenty year ago— no, damn near twenty-five, it was—I found me one. Right alongside this here road, it was. Bent over it, young feller. Lost me my billfold. He'd been beat up on. One of them gangland killings up from New York City. I just druv away, didn't want no part of it. Know what happens?"

"Listen, she—"

"The *po*-lice come and pick up my billfold. Call the old lady and say, 'Mrs. Heinlein, either your husband got himself kilt or he kilt a man.' Talk about killing, it damn near did the poor old lady in." His chuckle was a dry rasping sound and he rapped his bony knuckles against the cover of the true crime magazine. "Yessir, I could tell you a thing or two about finding bodies."

"She was bitten," I said, "by one of those dogs that got loose over near Mirror Lake."

He sprang to his feet. "Why'n't you say so?" As he picked up the telephone, I saw Les's silhouette through the glass of the door. When I opened it he carried Bunny inside and set her down on the chair. The girl driving with him came in right behind them with a plaid blanket and the two of them wrapped Bunny in it.

"Orin," she said. "Orin ..." With just the right amount of confusion and fear. Considering what she'd been through, she was amazingly good.

"Yop," the old man was shouting into the telephone. "Bitten by one of them there Eskimo dogs.... Yop, okay, sure." He hung up. "Keep her warm, the man said. And no spirits to drink."

Les looked up, startled. "Christ, I found a bottle of rum on the seat of your car and gave her a drink."

I shrugged and said, "Look, if it's shock they're worried about, hadn't we better get her to lie down?"

"Aren't you also supposed to elevate the feet higher than the head?" Les's girl asked. I nodded.

We eased Bunny down on the floor and wrapped her in the blanket again. The old man folded his mackinaw and placed it under her feet. That was when she let her eyelids flutter open and said, "Orin ... my husband ... back there...."

At first I became rattled, for we were supposed to wait as long as possible with that. But then I could hardly keep from smiling. She was magnificent. She was giving me the chance to get their bags where they belonged, but I still needed the trunk key.

"Please ..." she said, and I bent over her.

Her hand came up and I touched it. "It's going to be all right," I said. I could feel the keys she pressed into my palm. Wrapped up like that, I don't know how she got to them unless her mind had been chewing on it all along. I stood up. Les looked at me.

"You think she means her husband is still back there looking for her?" he asked.

"Could be. Stay with her. I'll take a look."

"Want me to go with you?"

"No, you better stay here in case anything happens."

Before he could answer, I went outside and a few seconds later was driving back to where the Kemp car was parked. I pulled up in front of it and quickly transferred the two suitcases to the trunk and locked it. Now what? I thought. Now I was supposed to look for him. But I didn't have to find him, did I?

I tramped up and down the shoulder of the road a few times. I even walked off thirty or forty yards into the timber, giving it ten minutes and then leaving Bunny's keys in the ignition lock of their car and driving back to the gas station in the Willys wagon. A state police patrol car, probably from the barracks outside of Jay, had just pulled in when I got there. Two cops in parkas and fur-lined hats with the ear flaps up climbed out. I followed them across the snow into the office.

It was perfect, I thought as I shut the door behind me. It was beautiful. What could go wrong?

Before long I was to start finding out what could go wrong and how far it could go wrong—like a stone wall collapsing on you.

CHAPTER FOURTEEN

"Find him?" Les asked.

"No. There wasn't anybody there."

One of the cops unbuttoned his parka and sat on his heels near Bunny. The folded handkerchief had clotted to her cheek with dried blood and he didn't try to remove it. He opened one of her eyes, grunted and felt her pulse. The other one said:

"Who found her, you, mister?" He was looking at Les.

"Not me. This guy."

The cop turned slowly to stare at me. "But you just now came in," he said, puzzled. He was young and tall and had that competent, self-assured look most of them get. Norstad, I remembered, had it too.

"She said something about her husband looking for her, so I went back to find him."

"And?"

I spread my hands out. "Nobody there."

"Where was it?"

"About a thousand yards back up the road toward Wilmington."

"Pulse seems okay," the other one said. "You say she got bit, Heinie?"

"The feller said," the old man told him.

"That's right, officer. I saw the tooth marks on her face. The handkerchief's covering them."

"Can't you do anything for her?" Les's girl asked.

Les patted her shoulder. "Take it easy, Helen."

The cop who'd examined Bunny said, "We already called Mirror Lake Memorial for an ambulance. It should be here before long, Miss."

"Why don't you tell us how it happened?" the tall, competent-looking cop asked me. "Could save yourself a trip to the barracks later."

"Sure, of course. I was driving along when I saw their car parked on the shoulder and—"

"Their car? I thought she was alone."

I shrugged, keeping my face frozen. Hell, I thought, just one question and I'd have sent the stylus rocketing off the drum on a polygraph. "I told you, didn't I, how she said something about her husband still being back there?"

"But you couldn't find him?"

"That's right."

"Okay, take it from the beginning, Mr.—"

"Odlum. I'm Chuck Odlum. My wife owns the Whiteface Hotel, where the dogs were lost. That's why I feel so bad about this."

"Mister," he said, his voice going suddenly frosty, "we're going to see you about those dogs. They're part wolf, aren't they? What right have you people got bringing them into the state at all? A little boy was attacked in Lake Placid, or didn't you know that? And now this."

I didn't mind him riding me about the dogs, for it got his mind off that slip about their car. I said, "The thing is, they're usually as tame as collies or chows or any breed you can name. As a matter of fact, they probably have more chow than wolf in them. But when they got loose they couldn't forage for themselves because they never had to before. Hunger can make any dog go wild."

"Okay, maybe I was a little out of line. What were you doing out in this storm anyway?"

"I dropped in on Deputy Moon in Lake Placid to talk about the dogs, then I was driving down to Plattsburg to see about a Poma lift for our ski slope at the Whiteface." I didn't like that question, though the answer seemed to satisfy him. That business of the dogs had riled him, I thought, or he wouldn't have asked that question. He wanted to lean on me.

He scowled and asked, "Driving down to Plattsburg in this weather?"

"Sure. Otherwise I'm all tied up with the hotel ski school. It's a one-man show. I run it."

"Go ahead."

"Well, I saw their car. I started to slow, and I saw her. She was coming out of the birches, sort of staggering. I stopped and got out just as she fell down.

I had to carry her back to the station wagon."

"You see the dog?"

"No, I don't think so."

"Did you or didn't you?"

"I heard it howling, officer," Helen said. Les looked at her but didn't contradict her.

"But you didn't get a look at it, Mr. Odlum?"

"No."

"Then what happened?"

"Well, these folks came along and helped me bring her here. That's about it."

"Anybody know her?"

Les shook his head. "We're on our way to Montreal from New York. We don't know anybody around here." I was about to say no, I didn't know her, but I checked myself. When they took her to the hospital they might trace her back to the Whiteface, or she might tell them she'd stopped there for several days.

"The funny part of it is," I said, "she looks familiar. She might have been a guest at the hotel, but I'm not sure. I don't pay much attention to that end of it, not unless they go out for the ski school."

"But you think you saw her there?"

"Yes, I think so." I scowled, looking down over the other cop's shoulder at her. "I'm almost sure."

He bought that with silence and a poker face. The other cop stood up then with Bunny's red leather wallet in his hand. "Driver's license," he said, going through it. "Made out to Bonita Kemp, and address in Long Island City, New York."

"Money?" the tall one asked.

"No currency. Just some silver in the change purse."

The tall one took off his fur-lined hat and ran a hand through sandy hair. "She wasn't traveling alone," he said, "not without money." He turned to me. "Is the name familiar, Mr. Odlum? Kemp?"

I thought I had taken it far enough. "No. No, I don't think so. I can tell you this much: she didn't sign up for the ski school."

The old man said, "Feller that walked with a limp, had a red face and glasses, come in here this morning for some gas."

"On foot?" the cop named Ed asked him.

"Yessir. Real gimpy leg. Said he was stuck without no gas down the road maybe half a mile. Gave him a can, five gallon can with two gallons high test in her. That's seventy cents for the gas, two bucks for the can. He ain't showed up."

Ed was buttoning his parka. "I better go have a look, Sarge," he said.

"Right. I'll join you down there when the ambulance gets here. I don't like that bad leg of his. He's liable to be in trouble."

Ed went out and a few seconds later I heard the patrol car start. When I looked at Bunny again, her eyes were open and she said, "I want my husband." Apparently she realized she couldn't carry a case of shock too far, for she couldn't fake the pallor, the cold sweat or the rapid, shallow heartbeat which were always symptomatic of it. "I want my husband," she said again, tonelessly, and tried to sit up.

The sergeant leaned over her and pushed gently on her shoulder. "Try to relax, ma'am. Everything's going to be all right. I'm a state policeman. How do you feel now?"

"What? Who ... are you?"

"I'm a state policeman, ma'am," he repeated patiently.

"The dog," Bunny said, her eyes widening. "Oh, God...."

"Don't talk about it now. Just take it easy, huh?"

"He said to wait in the car ... in the car."

"You weren't alone? Your husband was with you?"

"Orin. Yes."

"Man with a bad leg?"

"Please, it hurts."

The sergeant straightened up and paced around the little office restlessly while Les and Helen tried to comfort Bunny. She asked for a drink and Les brought it, tilting the glass of water to her lips and propping her head up so she could sip slowly. By now the sergeant could be reasonably sure that Orin Kemp was still out there, and his restlessness showed it.

About forty minutes after the cop named Ed had gone out looking for him, the ambulance came. Two men, one wearing a parka and the other a tweed suburban coat, brought a folded stretcher into the gas station office. The one in the suburban coat immediately knelt near Bunny and removed the stopper from a small flask and held it near her nose. Bunny began to cough and turned her head away. The intern checked her pulse, looked at her eyes and touched the handkerchief that was stuck to her cheek but didn't try to remove it. They opened the stretcher alongside her and got her on it. They hadn't said a word until then.

"Little or no shock," the intern said, standing up before they lifted the stretcher. "Sometimes it doesn't set in till later. Much exposure, sergeant?"

"Search me. We don't have the whole story yet."

"Well, will you get down to Mirror Lake as soon as you can and fill us in?"

"Right. Can she wait? There might be another one."

"Not with a face bite I wouldn't want her to wait," the intern said in a soft voice so Bunny wouldn't hear.

"You don't fool around with the possibility of infection that close to the brain."

It struck me for the first time that Bunny might be seriously hurt. I wanted to talk to her, to comfort her, but I couldn't of course. I watched the sergeant open the door and watched them take her outside on the stretcher through the snow.

"Can you give me a lift up the road a bit?" the sergeant asked.

"I'll take you," I said. "If her husband's still out there I want to help."

"We'd appreciate that, Odlum. Thanks."

They slid the stretcher in on its rack and slammed the rear door of the ambulance. The intern rode in back with her as the ambulance drove away. Through the glass door panels I could see him leaning over the stretcher.

Les and Helen joined us outside, and Les said, "Can we go back and help you look for him, sergeant? We never would have made it all the way through to Montreal in this blizzard anyway."

"You sure can, and thanks."

They got into their car and I climbed into the station wagon with the sergeant. "Name's Phil Walters," he said, slightly embarrassed. "I want to apologize about before, Okay?" He stuck out his hand and I shook it.

"Nothing to apologize about, Sergeant Walters. I don't blame you for being mad about those dogs."

Les and Helen followed us up the road to where the Kemp car was parked. The state trooper named Ed had pulled their patrol car up in front of it. The red dome light was blinking.

We parked and piled out. "Hey, Ed!" Sergeant Walters bawled into the wind. "Ed, where are you?"

After a while we saw him tramping down through

the birches. He pounded his gloved hands together and whistled, "What a blizzard," he said. "My fingers feel like they're ready to fall off."

"Any luck?"

Ed shook his head. "I've been up and down both sides of the road two hundred yards either way, maybe halfway up to the ridge on both sides. Can't find a trace of him."

"Suppose you show us where you found Mrs. Kemp, Odlum," Sergeant Walters told me.

I led them there. The wind and snow had covered the second set of tracks Bunny and I had made. "Right around here," I shouted above the shrieking of the wind. "She fell down just before I reached her."

"You didn't see any other tracks?"

"I didn't notice."

"Okay, here's what we'll do. Chances are if he's anyplace it's on this side of the road. Ed, you and Mr. Odlum go down the line toward the gas station and all the way up to the ridge if you have to. You think he could have cleared the ridge with a bum leg?"

"Not in a million years," Ed said. "I've been up there."

"You two," Sergeant Walters told Les and Helen, "take it back up the other way. And don't wander off too far." He grinned bleakly. "We wouldn't want you lost on us too. I'll take it straight up to the ridge line from here. All right, let's go. Give it half an hour, no matter what, and then check back at the cars."

He began to climb the hill. Les and Helen floundered up through the snow in the direction Orin Kemp had chased us nearly four hours ago and I went the other way with Ed. He told me to stay near the road while he angled up toward the ridge.

As I walked I beat my hands together for warmth. The wind came in howling gusts, driving me against the sloping boles of the birches. My legs trembled. I realized, then, that I was weak with fatigue and tension. I watched Ed slogging steadily through the snow. He waved once, shook his head, then pointed at his wrist to remind me to return in half an hour. Soon, except for an occasional glimpse, the timber hid him from sight. I went on, losing track of time, my feet painfully cold despite the double ski boots. When our half hour was up, I thought, Kemp would have been out here over four hours. And Bunny? By then Bunny would be nearing the hospital in Mirror Lake. I floundered in the deep snow and went down and got up covered with it from head to foot. Brushing myself off, I began to get the shakes. I pulled the drawstring sleeve of my ski jacket back and looked at my watch. Twenty minutes. Time to start back.

I met Ed on the way. He scowled and shook his head as we went the rest of the way together. Sergeant Walters was leaning in the open door of the patrol car, talking on the radio. I couldn't hear what he said. The wind-blown snow had buried the wheels of the patrol car on this side hub-cap deep.

Sergeant Walters straightened up. "Not a trace, huh?"

"Not a trace," Ed told him.

"What about the others?"

Ed pursed his lips and shrugged, then we saw a single figure struggling toward us through the snow from the south. It was Helen, and she was waving her arms frantically to get our attention. We ran up there and she cried breathlessly:

"We found him! We found him!"

"Where?"

"Come on. Les is with him."

I trailed behind them thinking, all right, brother,

this is it. We followed Helen's footprints at a slogging run. Pretty soon she dropped back behind us. I could hear her panting, but she was smiling a little too. She shouted something, I couldn't make out what. Following her trail, we'd angled up close to the ridge and went along for a few hundred yards parallel to it. Up ahead, I saw the cut where Bunny and I had gone up and over. And below it, Les was huddled over Orin Kemp's body.

He was covered with snow. Les had brushed it off his face—not Orin Kemp's angry red face now, but a ghastly bluish white. He had put his glasses back on. The lenses were twin white disks.

Les stood up. "He's alive," he said. "He's still alive."

They were words, just words. At first they didn't register. I stood there, all alone in the world of wind and snow and cold. Sergeant Walters nudged me impatiently. I became aware that he'd been shouting instructions.

"What? What did you say?"

"Help me grab his legs. Mister, you and Ed take the shoulders. Come on, easy does it."

"He may be injured," I said stupidly. "You can't move—"

"This is no skiing accident, Odlum. Let's go."

We lifted him. I stumbled and the leg I was holding came down stiffly and heavily. Sergeant Walters bit off a four-letter word, but then waited patiently while I took up my burden again. We began to move slowly through the snow, carrying him.

We were almost an hour returning to the car. That would make five hours, I thought. We could have saved some time by driving back up the road and taking him straight down at right angles to the ridge, but no one suggested it.

Helen was waiting in the patrol car with the door open. She got out quickly and they opened the back door and took Kemp in there. Ed pulled the door shut from the inside, staying with him. Sergeant Walters jumped behind the wheel and started the car. The rear tires spun and whined in the snow. They were snow tires with thick winter treads, but that didn't help.

"Christ!" Sergeant Walters shouted. "Give us a push."

I got behind the car with Les and we pushed, floundering in the snow and choking on the exhaust. Sergeant Walters stopped revving the engine when he saw it wasn't going to help. Rolling down the window, he said: "That wagon of yours four-wheel-drive?"

"Yeah."

"Let's move him."

We wrestled Kemp's body out of the patrol car and over to the station wagon. I dropped the tail gate and they carried him in that way. I have an old blanket in there. They wrapped him in it. Sergeant Walters pushed the gladstone bag over on its side, sitting on it, sitting on a hundred and seventeen thousand dollars, I thought, feeling the hysterical urge to laugh welling inside of me. Then Sergeant Walters leaned over Kemp. After a while he said, "Pulse so thready you can hardly feel it, but he's still alive all right. Ed, you put in a call and stay with the car. They'll give you a tow."

"Right, Sarge."

Les and Helen came up next to me in the snow.

"I want to thank you two," Sergeant Walters said.

"Don't be silly," Les told him, slightly embarrassed. "Anybody would have helped you. We just happened to be around. But will you be needing us anymore now?"

Sergeant Walters shook his head impatiently. He wanted to get started. I wanted Les to recite the soliloquy from *Hamlet* while we waited and listened to him. I felt light-headed, but desperate too. Kemp was still alive.

"Well," Les was saying, "if that bus of ours will get started, Helen and I thought we'd like to at least make it into Plattsburg for the night. Okay?"

"Of course it's okay. And thanks again."

"We'll call from Plattsburg and find out how he is. Poor guy. Mirror Lake Memorial Hospital, right?"

"Yes. Yes, it's the closest one." Sergeant Walters leaned forward on the gladstone bag and jerked his head at me. I swung the tail gate up and locked it.

Les and Helen had just reached their car when we started rolling.

"He's cold," Sergeant Walters said. "He's cold as ice, but he's breathing."

I shuddered and drove.

CHAPTER FIFTEEN

Three-quarters of an hour later we went up the receiving ramp of the Mirror Lake Memorial Hospital. It was a low, two-story brick and glass building with a modernistic facade and an acre of garden out front, snow-mantled now, laid out like a formal eighteenth-century garden. At one side of the ramp I saw a white ambulance parked. I wondered if they had brought Bunny here in it.

Sergeant Walters climbed over the front seat before I pulled the station wagon to a stop. He opened the door and went out running, calling back over his shoulder: "Get that tail gate down."

I did it, and in a minute two white-uniformed attendants came running up with a stretcher. One of them climbed in through the tail gate and the other slid the stretcher in. I helped them lift Kemp on it, then watched them carry him away.

I followed them inside, but they were moving faster than I was. I went along a rubber-tiled corridor with hospital green walls. It was warm in there and smelled of cleaning compound. I heard a bell, and a loudspeaker voice asked Dr. Somebody to report to surgery. An intern rushed past me, his tennis sneakers soundless on the rubber-tile floor.

Sergeant Walters stood lounging against the wall outside the door of the emergency room, his parka unbuttoned and the fur-lined hat in his hand.

"Smoke?"

"Thanks," I said, taking a cigarette from the crushproof box he offered me. We lit up and I asked, "How is he?"

"Too early to tell. He's cold, though, I can tell you that. We've had cases here where the body temperature drops to eighty degrees or less, and some of them pull through. Deep shock's the main thing you have to worry about. And complications."

"Like pneumonia?"

"Like pneumonia." Sergeant Walters sucked in a deep drag and let the smoke trickle out through his nostrils. Then he took another puff, blew the smoke out and punched me on the shoulder. "You're all right, Odlum. You and those folks out there. I never even got their name. Some cop, huh? But what I mean is, it's a pretty ugly line of work most of the time, until some good Samaritans come along and then you feel, what the hell, everything's worthwhile." Color flooded his hard, competent face. "Hell, I talk too much."

We stood smoking in silence. Just how much interest could I show him? I wondered. I said, figuring he'd buy this much anyway, "How's the woman?" On top of everything else, I was almost crazy with worry about Bunny.

He shrugged. "Haven't checked. She ought to be okay, though. Whether her husband pulls through or not, that's something else again." Ash dropped off his cigarette on the rubber-tiled floor. He put the butt out in a standing ashtray. "Want a hot cup of coffee? I've got drag around here."

"I could be talked into it," I said. We grinned at each other and went downstairs to the staff cafeteria, where we each had two cups of coffee, black, and then some crullers with a third cup. Sergeant Walters made small talk with a couple of nurses he knew. With the warmth and the coffee, the tension began to grow in me again. What if Kemp lived? What if he talked? Out in the snow, I thought he had mistaken me for Norstad, but that didn't make any difference. He might rave, deliriously, how his wife had run off with Norstad, leaving him to die in the snow. He might rave about the money.

"... give you a ring one of these days," Walters was saying to a moon-faced nurse with pretty eyes.

"Well, I won't hold my breath, Sarge."

"Ah, go on."

The other nurse told me, smiling, "He's been threatening call her up for six months now."

"I'm the shy type," Walters said. "I get stage fright every time I go near the phone."

"The tall, silent, deadly type," the moon-faced nurse said. "That's the type I go for."

They batted it around for a while, laughing at their

own banter and stale jokes more than was warranted, I thought. Or maybe that was just the way I felt. For Walters, the tension was over. He could afford to relax. For me it was just beginning.

Finally Walters stood up. "I didn't know you could cook too, Margie. Those crullers were out of this world."

"There's lots of things about me you don't know."

"Well," Walters told me, "let's take a look at the patient."

We went back upstairs to the emergency room. Walters peeked in through the Judas window set high in the swinging door. "They're still working on him."

I nodded. I didn't want to look.

"Got him in an oxygen tent."

"Pneumonia?"

"Probably that's what they're afraid of. Hey, here comes the doc."

The door swung out and a white-uniformed intern came through it. His hair was dark and streaked with premature gray. He wore shell-rimmed glasses and his lips were pursed in thought.

"How's his chances?" Walters asked.

The intern showed us his hand horizontal to the floor, first with the palm down then with the palm up. "It could go either way. There was a case in Chicago once a few winters back that made all the medical journals. A Negress, stewed to the gills and out all night in subzero temperature. They brought her in with a rectal reading of sixty-nine degrees, and she pulled through. But half the time they go out on you at eighty degrees, and in that case the alcohol didn't help, either. You just can't figure it."

"What about Kemp?"

"Seventy-six degrees. We've got him wrapped in electric blankets, we've shot him full of anticoagulants to keep his blood moving and antibiotics to fend off pneumonia. He's in an oxygen tent and we gave him 1-arterinol because his blood pressure is way down."

"Never mind the medical gobbledygook, doc. How's his chances?"

"Well, if his body doesn't start building up its own heat in the next few hours, he's finished. And even if it does, he's in deep shock. And if he manages to survive that, we'll have to sweat out fulminating pneumonia."

"In other words, not so hot?"

"One in five at best. He's got a long uphill fight. How'd he get caught out there in the blizzard, anyhow?"

"I wish to hell I knew," Walters said, frowning. "Car went out of gas on him, so he hikes down the road to a station, brings a can back and wanders off into the timber. The only thing I can figure, this dog was chasing his wife and he lit out after them. She's hysterical, the dog gets scared off, she wanders back to the road and this man here finds her. But hell, if his life depended on it he would have been able to drag himself down to the road, bum leg or no, wouldn't he?"

The intern shook his head. "I forgot to tell you. His left ankle's badly sprained, swollen like a balloon. And he has a simple fracture of the right tibia. He couldn't have dragged himself anywhere."

"The poor slob," Walters said. "What about his wife?"

"The bite they brought in earlier? She's lucky. Not much exposure and just mild shock." I held my breath listening. "Had to put sixteen stitches in her face, though. She'll have quite a scar until she can have it worked on by a plastic surgeon."

"Can I talk to her?" Walters asked.

"Well, I wish you wouldn't. We have her under light sedation. Tomorrow, sergeant?"

"Okay, there's no rush. I'd better phone in."

The intern nodded and went down the hall. Walters looked at me and stuck out his hand. I shook it. "Guys like you make this job worthwhile, Odlum," he said, fumbling for words. "I just wanted you to know that."

I smiled at him. "Can I give you a lift?"

"No, I guess I'll stay overnight."

I turned and walked away. I couldn't get away from him fast enough suddenly.

There was still something I had to do before I went back to the hotel. When I got outside, dusk had fallen, slate gray and dismal with the snow and wind. I backed the station wagon down the receiving ramp and picked up Route 86 between Mirror Lake and Lake Placid and drove along it to the secondary road which led to the Whiteface ski slope. I parked outside the lodge and brought the gladstone bag in there, unlocking the door of the storeroom and putting it inside. It would be all right there, I thought, for I had the only key and no one would go near the lodge in this storm anyway. And, when it was over, I'd be the boy to get the ski slope in shape.

One chance in five, I thought, locking up. Lousy odds for him, but they weren't great odds for us, either.

Run? It was an impulse, but not a very strong one. I had the money, but there was Bunny. Besides, the way I saw it, no one—not even Kemp if he lived—could tie me to the money except Bunny.

Driving back to the hotel I thought it was funny, in a way, about the money. A hundred and seventeen thousand bucks. I had it. I'd stored it away but I hadn't even opened the straps of the gladstone to look at it. What did a hundred and seventeen thousand bucks in small bills look like? The thing was, the money didn't mean much without Bunny. It was mine and hers, and I'd wanted her before I even knew it existed.

Just before I reached Route 86 I rolled down the window and tossed Kemp's gun into a stand of pine where the snow had drifted deep. Then I drove on to the Whiteface and parked outside, plodding stiffly through the snow, bone weary, to the main entrance.

CHAPTER SIXTEEN

It was Saturday night cocktail hour. As I came in I could hear Wally Shevlin's band playing a Latin American medley in the lounge. A couple of guests cornered me in the lobby to ask about the chances of skiing tomorrow, but I told them it would be Monday at least before I got the slopes ready—if it stopped snowing. Elaine Skinner was holding down the desk, but she didn't smile and didn't acknowledge my wave. I climbed the stairs, realizing how utterly exhausted I was. An hour of sleep this morning was all I'd had since Thursday night, and this morning seemed like a year or two ago.

I turned the handle of our door. It was locked. I knocked. No answer. I liked the idea of not having to face Inez now. All I wanted to do was sleep. Getting out my key, I inserted it in the lock. It wouldn't turn.

What the hell, I thought. The key went in all right, but it wouldn't budge. I looked up at the room number. No mistake. Inez and I slept in 201, at the top of the stairs on the second floor.

A chambermaid came by with a dustpan and a broom. She gave me an embarrassed smile, as if she knew something I didn't know, and hurried on. I went downstairs and across the lobby to the desk.

"Where's Hank?" I asked Elaine. Hank was the Whiteface handyman.

"Around. I don't know where."

"Well, can you call him on the P.A.?"

Then I saw the look on Elaine's face. She was mad. "If you want me to," she said coldly. "But it won't do any good."

"What gives?"

"You're locked out, isn't that the trouble? I know because I put the work order through. Mrs. Cameron made it out."

I didn't say anything right away. A year and a half ago, before Inez came back from Miami, Elaine and I had an affair. Just for kicks, I'd thought, with no scent of orange blossoms in the air. Elaine had dropped it as lightly as I had after Inez and I had started going around together. There hadn't been any cooling-off period or any awkward readjustment, and since then Elaine had been an efficient social director with a strictly hands-off-the-married-merchandise attitude.

"Look," Elaine said, "I organize games and I get people together at dances. I'm the professional maiden-aunt type and that's okay with me. I even like it. But there was an ugly scene today and I almost lost my job, and that I don't like."

"What are you talking about?"

"Mrs. Cameron accused me of having an affair with you. Present tense." Elaine smiled wryly. "At least if I had the game as well as the name."

"Huh?" I said stupidly. "I'm dense I guess. You'll have to spell it out."

"Don't mind that last crack, Chuck. Chalk it up to overwork or anything you want. But okay, I can spell it out for you. Danny Giardello popped up this morning. He saw the vet in Lake Placid and got the lowdown on the huskies, He talked himself into a job feeding them and taking care of them and, if the huskies get along with him, even running the dogsled rides. Kirby Rowe went for the idea and hired him on the spot. Danny's a nice kid."

"Yeah. So what?" Danny Giardello was the Lake Placid teenager who helped out around the ski slopes.

"So his gal-friend spent the afternoon here."

"I still don't get it."

"Well, until my maidenly virtues, such as they are, enter the scene, I get the rest of this second hand. Marie—that's the gal-friend—was trying to impress people what a big wheel her Danny is. The trouble was, she didn't recognize Mrs. Cameron. Do you begin to get the picture now, lover boy?"

"I'm still way out in left field. And cut out the sarcasm, will you?"

"Yesterday Danny caught you with lipstick all over your face at the lodge. He must have told Marie. It impressed her. It meant her Danny was like this with the husband of the Whiteface owner." Elaine crossed the index and middle fingers of her left hand. "Only, Marie's not too bright. She had to talk about it. In her eyes it made the boyfriend a big wheel. The trouble was, she chose Mrs. Cameron as her sounding board.

"The first I knew of it, Mrs. C wanted me to pack my lures and get out. I was the obvious candidate, wasn't I? We had a little scene, with Kirby Rowe all ears. From where I stand, it looks like Inez confided in him. Anyway, I was able to prove I never left the hotel yesterday, which left me out. Then, later, the work order came through." She added:

"Would you like a single room, Mr. Odlum? We have a very nice single on the third floor."

"Ah, cut it out," I said. I felt light headed and woozy with the need for sleep. I tried to think what this would mean for me and Bunny, but I couldn't hold onto a train of thought long enough to decide if it would help us or hurt us. I surprised Elaine by saying: "All right, I'll take it."

She bit her lip and took down a key from the mail board and gave it to me. "Who's the lucky girl?" The crazy thing was, I realized suddenly, Elaine was jealous. She'd never given a sign of it when I married Inez. It took what must have looked to all of them, to her and Inez and Kirby Rowe, like a casual roll in the hay to get her goat. Dames, I thought. Try and figure them.

"Keep it under your hat," I said. "It's Mrs. Ohls." Mrs. Ohls was the handyman's wife, a stolid, unsmiling dish at sixty years old.

"Oh, get out of here," Elaine said, and I did.

I went into the lounge. Wally Shevlin smirked at me from the bandstand and rolled his eyes. In a resort hotel like the Whiteface, a thing like that gets around. I could picture Hank Ohls gumming his plates into place and telling how he'd changed the lock on our room. Inez would have everything she needed for a divorce action but the correspondent. I had to repeat it to myself until I got it: the correspondent. That would look great, I thought, if she could tie me to Bunny like that, for Sergeant Walters would remember I hadn't even been sure if Bunny had stayed at the hotel when I found her in the snow. I felt cold all over. Was there any way Inez could pin it on Bunny? I told myself to relax. How could she?

At the bar Sammy said, "Hiya, Chuck. Where ya been?" He gave me a knowing grin. "Man, you look beat. Like you just got back from a twenty-four-hour honeymoon."

"Give me a double bourbon on the rocks," I said, not smiling.

He poured the drink. "No kidding, where ya been?"

"Read about it in tomorrow's paper."

"Honest?" He looked surprised.

"Honest. I'm a hero."

I put the drink down in two gulps and set the glass on the bar and got out of there. Looking at the number on my room key, I took the elevator up to the third floor. It was room 305, where Bunny had stayed. I took off my ski boots and jacket, dropped on the bed with the rest of my clothes on and fell into an exhausted sleep.

CHAPTER SEVENTEEN

Toward dawn I had a nightmare. I was in an oxygen tent at the hospital and all these faces came crowding together to stare at me accusingly through the polyethylene walls. They came closer and closer and I couldn't get away. Kemp was there, and Sergeant Walters and Bunny, Inez and Kirby Rowe and even the deputy sheriff, Joe Moon. Then all the faces swam together and this one giant face of Orin Kemp moved in through the polyethylene.

I came out of it gasping and drenched with sweat. Gray pre-dawn light framed the window shade. I got up, went into the bathroom and sloshed ice-cold water on my face, then smoked a cigarette sitting on the edge of the bed. It was a quarter to six. When I finished the cigarette I tried to sleep again, but kept tossing and turning and worrying about Kemp. If he died, I had murdered him. If he lived, I could kiss Bunny goodbye, for if he hadn't seen me out there on the snow he certainly had seen Bunny.

After a while it grew lighter. I decided I could call the hospital once this morning without arousing suspicion. But not at six o'clock I couldn't. Somehow I had to get through the next couple of hours. I could have killed some time showering and shaving, but didn't have a change of clothes or a razor. I had three more cigarettes, staring up at the ceiling and watching the smoke drift.

At a little before seven I picked up the phone and asked for room 201.

Inez's voice. "Yes? This is Mrs. Cameron."

"Chuck, Inez. Could I come down there after some stuff?"

"... give me a few minutes to get dressed."

I waited a while and then went downstairs to the second floor. I knocked on the door.

"It isn't locked."

She was seated at her vanity table combing her hair. I saw her face in the mirror, drawn and dramatic looking, fine boned, like the face of an expensive fashion model. She turned around slowly on the vanity bench. She was wearing a black velvet bolero over a white blouse and black velvet lounging slacks. The skin of her face was a rich tan from the sunlamp.

"I don't want to fight with you, Chuck," she said. "I just want to ask you one question."

"Okay, shoot."

"I can take anything, I guess, except another woman." You could tell it was hurting her to say that. "Chuck, is there another woman?"

"You seemed pretty sure of it last night."

"I said I didn't want to argue with you. You've humiliated me as it is. I can hardly show my face around the hotel."

"If you know all the answers, why ask me?"

"What else could I think? Danny Giardello's girl said—"

"I know what she said. I know how you gave Elaine a hard time."

"There was three hundred dollars missing from the safe. I didn't take it. Kirby Rowe didn't. You're the only other person who knows the combination. I … I assumed you went to Plattsburg with her yesterday, to buy her something with the money. But then I heard the news broadcast from Plattsburg last night."

I waited, hardly breathing. What had they said about Orin Kemp?

"If there was another woman, you weren't with her yesterday. Now I don't know what to think."

"What about the newscast?"

"I don't have to tell you. You know what you did. I … you want to hear something funny …? I was very proud of you. Chuck, I want you to tell me if there's another woman."

"You mean, besides Elaine?"

Her face darkened under the tan. "I guess I deserved that."

I stood there, not talking. Take it slow, I thought. Do you want to tell her there's another woman? That's the best reason for leaving, and whatever happens to Kemp you're going to have to leave. But would Inez let it lie? I didn't think so. If I admitted that much, she'd want to know who it was. She'd move heaven and earth to find out who it was. And if that happened, if she could tie me to Bunny, we wouldn't just leave. We'd run.

"I'm waiting, Chuck."

If I denied the whole thing? I looked at Inez's dark,

fine-boned face. It was anxious and vulnerable. She sat there, absolutely still, her eyes on mine, waiting for my answer. If I chalked it all up to an over-worked imagination on the part of Danny's girl, she'd believe me. She wanted to believe me.

The telephone rang. Inez went over to the bed and sat down on the edge, picking up the receiver that was on the night table. "Yes? This is Mrs. Cameron speaking.... No, I'll see you later.... I don't know. I'll see you later, I said.... I don't know anything of the kind for sure." She hung up and looked at me.

"What does Kirby think?" I asked.

"All right, that was Kirby. You're very perceptive. But don't you see, he's the only friend I have if you...."

"I see he's ready to pick you up, when you bounce."

"Chuck."

"The always available Mr. Rowe. Waiting, on call, for you and your hotel."

"That's unfair."

"He's never stopped trying, has he?"

"He hasn't come near me since we were married."

"Who's that man I saw you with yesterday while I out making like a hero?"

"Must you turn everything into a filthy joke? Must you?"

"Look, Inez. You said you didn't want to fight with me. I came down here for some toilet articles and a change of clothes. All right?"

"If that's the way you want it."

She stood up and waited, stiffly, her fists clenched at her sides, while I got my razor, shaving cream and tooth brush from the bathroom and an armful of clothes from the closet and bureau. I knew it was my fault. I felt hot under the collar, but I didn't want to talk to anyone, least of all Inez. I just wanted to wait until I could call the hospital, and find out what was happening, and begin to make plans. I stomped out of there, not looking at her. Inez slammed the door.

Upstairs, I showered and shaved, dawdling, stretching it out. By the time I dressed it was seven-forty. I went downstairs to the dining room after some breakfast, not hungry but knowing I had to eat. I found an empty table as far across the room as I could get from where Inez and Kirby Rowe would be eating. I saw Kirby over there, eating alone. I didn't see Inez. The griddle cakes and bacon tasted like straw.

I called the Mirror Lake Memorial Hospital from the pay booth in the lobby. Three rings, then:

"Mirror Lake Memorial. One moment please."

The line went dead. The switchboard was busy. I sat in the booth, sweating.

"Yes, sir? May I help you, sir?"

"This is Mr. Odlum over at the Whiteface. Yesterday I—"

"Oh yes, Mr. Odlum. All of us here know what you did yesterday. The Mirror Lake community is very proud of you," the switchboard girl said warmly, possessively. "Have you seen the *Plattsburg Times* this morning?"

"No, I—"

"But here I am ranting like this when you want to know about the Kemps. I'll connect you."

The line went dead again, then another voice said: "Emergency, Mrs. Himmel. May I help you?"

"This is Chuck Odlum over at the Whiteface. I was wondering if you could tell me about the couple we brought in yesterday?"

"Mr. Kemp responded to treatment," she said, and I felt my heart jump. "During the night his body temperature returned to normal, but unfortunately, toward morning, pneumonia set in."

"Bad?"

"Fulminating pneumonia, Mr. Odlum. He hasn't regained consciousness as yet. He's on the critical list."

"He going to live?"

"I'm sorry, but I can offer no prognosis. You'd have to see Dr. Holland in person."

"What about the woman?"

"Mrs. Kemp? She isn't in Emergency. I'll connect you."

I thought she'd connect me with the floor nurse where Bunny was, but then I heard Bunny's voice. "Hello?"

I thought fast. I didn't want her to make any mistakes. "Hello," I said, "is this where they have Mrs. Kemp? This is Mr. Odlum calling."

I heard her suck in her breath. "This is Mrs. Kemp talking," she said, and I knew it was going to be all right.

"Maybe you don't know me, Mrs. Kemp, but yesterday I helped them bring you and your husband in. How are you this morning?"

"They told me what you did, Mr. Odlum. I don't know how to thank you. But I know you, of course. I remember you from the hotel."

"How're you feeling, Mrs. Kemp?"

"I'm all right. They're going to let me out of here tomorrow. Then I'll want to see you and thank you for what you did."

I figured they hadn't told her about Kemp, because she was a patient too. I said, "I'm sorry about your husband."

"... they won't tell me anything about him. Is he hurt bad?" Her voice rose. "Is he—"

"I guess I should have kept my big mouth shut. You

better check with the doctor."

"No. Please. I want you to tell me."

"Well, he developed pneumonia. He's on the critical list."

"Thank you. I'm glad you told me. They treat you like a baby in the hospital. I want to see him. I'm going to make them let me see him."

"Well, good luck, Mrs. Kemp."

"Goodbye. And thank you again."

"Goodbye."

I hung up and opened the folding door. I took two steps, congratulating myself because the call had come off so well, when I saw him coming across the lobby toward me. A big, competent-looking guy. Norstad.

"Mr. Odlum, isn't it?" he said. He had a newspaper tucked under his arm.

"Yes, that's right, Mr. Norstad."

He tapped the newspaper. "I see where you found him for me."

I almost said something like I guess I did at that, but I caught myself. I wouldn't have known Orin Kemp was the man he was looking for, would I? "Found him?" I asked. "Found who?"

"Kemp. The guy I was after?"

"Hell," I said, "you mean to say Kemp's your pigeon?"

"He sure is. Lucky I decided against driving up to Saranac Lake through the storm."

"It still snowing?" I hadn't even looked outside.

"No, I mean last night. It finally stopped. Fifty-three inches, the paper said."

"We get that up here every few years."

"It would paralyze them downstate for a week."

"Up here we're used to it. Plows'll have the road clear by tonight. By the morning for sure."

"Amazing," he said, shaking his head. Then he went

on into the dining room.

All of a sudden it got hold of me. I'd called him by name. But he hadn't ever told me his name, had he? I tried to remember but couldn't. The only thing I could come up with was a probable negative answer. I didn't remember him telling me his name, but I just wasn't sure. Would he make anything of it? I felt this cold chill, like before you come down with the flu. What the hell, I told myself, don't get yourself in an uproar. Why should he remember whether he told you his name or not? But he was a cop, even if he'd come up here to collect a hundred and seventeen thousand bucks for himself. And cops were trained to remember things like that. So what? I could have got his name from the hotel register.

I went over to the desk. Kirby Rowe sat there going over the reservation blanks. He looked up and nodded coldly, then ignored me. I turned the guest book around and ran my finger down the names. They blurred and swam together and I had to go through them three times before I could be sure.

There were a couple of dozen male singles since the middle of the week. None of them was Norstad. None of them came from Putnam County.

He'd used a phony name.

The only way I could have learned his name was from Bunny or Orin Kemp.

Kirby Rowe said something. I nodded, staring at him stupidly, and walked away.

Somehow I got through the rest of the morning.

CHAPTER EIGHTEEN

After lunch I got into my ski clothes and drove up to the lodge. I didn't want to think of Orin Kemp in the hospital and maybe talking, and I didn't want to think of Norstad and the slip I'd made. I tried to tell myself if he'd caught it the next move was his, not mine, but that didn't help. I just wanted to get away by myself and work until I was ready to drop from exhaustion.

A big yellow cat, its huge tires turning ponderously, was pushing a snowplow along Route 86. It had come this way before, because the plow's steel blade clattered and struck sparks off bare concrete. But the secondary road leading up to the lodge hadn't been touched. That was all right with me: you'd need four-wheel-drive to get through to the lodge, so I wouldn't be bothered with company.

I parked in front of the lodge and went inside, unlocking the door of the supply room to get a pair of skis. I saw the gladstone, its leather bulging with all that money. I stood looking at it a minute, then dropped to my knees and unfastened the straps and punched the snap release. The bag sprang open.

It was like a beautiful dream.

Maybe once the money had been stacked neatly in there. And maybe underneath, where I couldn't see them, there were stacks with tote bands around them. What I saw was money. Heaps of money, crumpled and stuffed and crammed and piled in. Some of it spewed out on the floor when the bag opened and the pressure on it let go. Gray and green bills, piles of them. Windrows of ten- and twenty-dollar bills. I dug my left hand in almost to the elbow and felt the hard neat stacks underneath. I picked the loose bills off the floor and crammed them back in. I studied a few of them at random. Federal Reserve Bank of Richmond, Virginia. Federal Reserve Bank of Atlanta, Georgia. Of New York. Series E. Series B. Series F. A hundred and seventeen thousand bucks, worn and rumpled and out of series. I closed the bag. I had to sit on it to make the lock snap, and then I saw a couple of the bills were sticking out. I opened it again, stuffed them in, shut it. I fastened the straps. My fingers were trembling.

For a minute I had this wild urge to pick up the bag and run. Then I thought of Bunny, waiting too as I was waiting, while her husband lingered between life and death in the hospital. If I didn't know it before, I knew now how much I loved her. The money was mine and Bunny's. I started daydreaming of how we would spend it, not crazily on a drunken spree the way Sloan and Hannah Howard had done, but carefully at first, feeding it into a business out West, building the business and maybe after a few years selling it if we wanted, then seeing the world together and later settling down with another business if we wanted, and all the time Bunny knowing I could have run out on her but hadn't, and loving....

Nuts, I thought; you're not out of the woods yet.

I took a pair of skis outside, clamped the bindings and started up the slope. I sidestepped down all afternoon, watching the world tilt and swing under the cold, cloudless blue sky as I worked. Then, towards dusk, I took two runs down from the top, crouching into the icy bite of the wind, feeling the smooth sliding speed and then swerving and cutting into a parallel Christie just this side of the station wagon and coming to a clean, snow-spewing stop. For a few minutes then

I was away from it, but after the second downhill run I heard the phone ringing in the lodge.

I took off my skis, went in there and picked up the receiver.

"Yeah?"

"I thought that's where I'd find you, Chuck." It was Elaine Skinner's voice. "Somebody wants to talk to you."

Before I could ask her who, another voice came on the line. "Odlum? This is Sergeant Walters."

I hadn't caught my breath yet, and now I could feel a pulse pounding in my throat. "Hi," I said. "I didn't know you'd still be around Mirror Lake."

"Well, we had to bring the Kemp car in. And I'll be damned if they didn't have to treat one of my hands for frostbite. How you making it?"

"Got no kicks. What about the Kemps?"

"Well, that's why I called you. Orin Kemp died this afternoon. Fulminating pneumonia takes them fast like that. A damn shame, huh?"

"It sure is." Kemp, I thought. Kemp was the last link. We were in.

"What I wanted to tell you, they'll be holding an inquest in Lake Placid, probably Monday afternoon or Tuesday, depending on when the coroner finishes with him. You'll have to testify."

"Sure, of course."

"Tell you what I'll do. I'll pass the word along to Joe Moon. You know him, the deputy?"

I said I knew him.

"He'll let you know when. Okay?"

"Okay. His wife know?"

"They told her. She's broken up about it, but she's a real trooper. She was with him when he died. She'll be all right. Well, I'll see you at the inquest."

"Right."

"You see the papers? They made a couple of heroes out of both of us."

"I'll start a scrapbook."

He laughed and I laughed and we hung up.

Kemp was dead. Sure, the inquest would mean a delay of twenty-four hours or so, but what difference did that make? Who said we weren't out of the woods yet?

When I returned to the hotel, everyone was talking about the huskies, for two of them had found their way back to the kennels. I went right over there and helped Danny Giardello feed them. At first they looked mean, growling and keeping their distance, but when we put out the horse meat for them they yelped and went at it eagerly.

After dinner I asked Inez if I could borrow her key to move the rest of my stuff upstairs. What I wanted to do was pack a bag in case I had to leave in a hurry, because I was still sweating Norstad out. I'd found Inez in the lounge, nursing a Benedictine and brandy alone at a corner table. I knew something was up, for Inez hardly drank at all.

"Would you like something to drink?"

"No, thanks."

We sat there silently. Several times she started to say something, then changed her mind. Finally it came out in a rush of words. "I did everything I could to make a go of our marriage, Chuck. I even kept the Whiteface open this winter because I knew you wanted that. And I never threw it in your face that I owned the place, did I? Did I, Chuck?"

"No, of course not."

"But it just isn't going to work out for us, is it? What's the sense of kidding ourselves? We can't go on the way we are."

I didn't say anything.

She lit a cigarette, took one puff and immediately put it out. She sipped the rest of her drink, sighed and said, "I want a divorce, Chuck."

I felt nothing, no pity, no regret. For a long time we'd just been going through the motions. "All right."

"I hope we're going to be adult about it. I hope you'll see it my way. Because I don't have the time or the inclination to go out of state for one of those assembly line divorces."

"Hold on a minute," I said. "The only grounds for divorce in New York State is adultery."

"I know. I want you to tell me who the girl is, then we can go ahead. Kirby says—"

"Oh, so it's Kirby is it? I didn't know he practiced law on the side," I said sarcastically.

"Kirby giving me advice has nothing to do with it. I'll need the girl's name as correspondent."

"I never said there was any girl."

"It's pretty obvious, isn't it, after what Danny Giardello saw up at the lodge?"

"Look, Inez. If you want a divorce I won't contest it, but you better buy yourself a plane ticket out to Reno or Arkansas or one of those other places where they grant a divorce because your husband gets hair oil on the antimacassars or lets his Doberman chew at the table legs or whatever else comes under the heading of mental cruelty."

"Oh? Is that right?"

"Yeah. You won't have any grounds for a New York action."

Inez gave me a nasty look. "There are ways to get grounds. I had hoped you'd act like a grownup, but I guess that was too much to hope for. Kirby said—"

"Ah, hell, Inez. Just give me the key." We'd just go round and round, I thought, so there was no sense in arguing with her. Obviously, I could never give her what she wanted. And I knew I'd have to watch my step with Bunny. Get out of the state, I thought. Meet out West somewhere. The hell with you, Inez.

She slammed the key down on the table between us. I took it and went upstairs and packed a bag, then brought it up to the third floor. Just as I put it in the closet, there was a knock at the door. I opened it and saw Inez standing there. She didn't try to come in. I didn't invite her in.

"As soon as we find a ski instructor to finish out the season," she said, "I want you out of here."

"Yes, ma'am, Mrs. Cameron."

"With two weeks' pay, just like you wanted to give Jack McCall."

"Yes, ma'am." I gave her the key. She took it, her eyes brimming with tears of rage, and shut the door between us hard so I wouldn't see her crying. I heard her high heels beat out an angry tattoo down the hall.

There are ways to get grounds, she had told me. I should have remembered that.

CHAPTER NINETEEN

Bunny called me the first thing in the morning.

"It's me," she said, not mentioning any name. "I'm out."

"Okay." I didn't like talking to her on the hotel phone because the PBX operator might have kept the line open.

"I have to see you. I'm at a luncheonette in Lake Placid called Mom's Place."

"I'll be there in twenty minutes."

I went downstairs and drove to Lake Placid in the station wagon. It was another clear cold day, but a strong wind blew off the lake. I parked in the Marcy lot and went across the street. I could see some kids shoveling snow off the lake to make an ice-skating rink.

I opened the door and went into Mom's Place. Behind the counter on one long wall two waitresses were talking together. A couple of skiers in bright sweaters, their jackets hanging on a hook, were having breakfast at the first booth on the other long wall. Bunny was waiting with a cup of coffee at the last booth before the juke box in back. I put a couple of dimes in the juke box and jabbed buttons at random. The juke gizmo clicked and went into action, moving a record. A rock-and-roll number began to blast. One of the waitresses gave me a dirty look.

When I sat down across the table from Bunny, I saw the bandage on her face. It was held in place, covering her right cheek, by adhesive tape. The bruise on her other cheek had turned yellowish. I looked at those eyes of hers and felt a lump in my throat because she'd been through so much I hadn't been able to help her with. She put her hand on the table and smiled at me. I covered her hand with mine.

"Hello," she said. "Hello."

"Bunny, I—"

"Don't talk. I just want to look at you. In the hospital I had a crazy idea I'd never see you again."

The waitress came over.

"Coffee," I said. "And toast."

"White or wheat?"

"White."

She went away.

"He never regained consciousness, Chuck. He never said a word."

"We're in, baby."

"I know."

"Does it hurt?"

"Only when I smile."

"Then don't."

"I have to smile, the way I feel."

"My wife asked for a divorce."

She squeezed my hand. "Then after a while we'll be able to get married."

"A New York divorce."

"That's impossible."

"I told her. Don't worry, she'll come around."

"I'm not worrying. I wasn't even counting on marriage." Bunny smiled a little. "They don't have to perform any ceremony to make me feel married to you."

The waitress came with my coffee and toast. She refilled Bunny's coffee cup from the silex and went back to the counter.

"Listen, I better tell you," I said. "Norstad's back at the hotel. He told me how I'd found his pigeon for him and I made a mistake. I called him by name."

"So what? Isn't he registered?"

"Not under his own name, he's not. I can't be sure, but I don't think he ever told me his name. The only way I could have learned it was from you or your husband."

Bunny sipped her coffee. "I wouldn't worry about that. A man gets called by name twenty times a day every day of his life. It wouldn't have meant a thing to Norstad,"

"He's a cop, with a cop's mind."

"Well, we can't do anything about it now."

"It's one more reason we can't be seen together. Do you have the car?"

"Yes. In the lot across the street."

"We'll have to set you up in a motel someplace till after the inquest. I know a little place out on the road to Lake Saranac. The Fawn Ridge Lodge. You go out there alone and stay there. Just stay put. You can let the sheriff's substation in Lake Placid know where you are so they can call you for the inquest, but that's all. Otherwise, drop out of sight and stay out of sight."

"All right. Take it easy."

"I saw the money, baby. I opened the bag and looked at it. It's ours and I want it to stay ours."

"Where did you put it?"

"In the lodge."

"That's what I had to see you about. The money. In the first place, just in case your slip does mean something to Norstad, I'd better take it out to the motel with me."

"I don't know."

"If I'll be safe there, the money will be safe there."

I lit a cigarette and nodded, knowing she was right. Besides, with things the way they were between me and Inez, she might even decide to have Danny Giardello take over the ski school until a permanent replacement turned up. That would be just great, with Danny poking around at the lodge.

"Good," Bunny said. "Then it's settled. Also, I need some money. Orin had just a little over seventy dollars on him and the hospital gave me a bill for over two hundred. Then there's the undertaker who's making arrangements to send the body by train down to Long Island City. I had the undertaker call Orin's brother. You see, they have a family burial plot out on Long Island. The undertaker's going to cost money too."

"Christ," I said, "I haven't thirty bucks to my name."

"Silly. You just have a hundred and seventeen thousand dollars."

"Can't you touch your brother-in-law for the money?"

"Him? Last I heard he was unemployed. I'll probably have to wire him the fare up here."

"I don't like the idea of spending any of that money here."

"What's the difference? We have to start spending it sooner or later, don't we? You can't always be afraid to spend it. It's perfectly safe, Chuck. You saw it, didn't you?"

I put my cigarette out and finished my coffee. "Yeah, I guess so. Don't mind me. I never had a crack at a hundred grand before, that's all. I was thinking you could send them a check or a money order later, after we got settled somewhere, but that's no good because Norstad might show the undertaker his buzzer and trace us. And a bum debt's just as bad."

"Then that's settled too. Where are we going, Chuck—after it's all over?"

"I don't know yet. Out West eventually. I could meet you in Albany or someplace. We'll work out the arrangements later. And look. Don't call me at the hotel unless you absolutely have to. I'll meet you right here after the inquest."

Bunny shook her head. "That's no good. Orin's brother, remember? I'll have to drive down to Long Island for the funeral. Make it the end of the week. I couldn't get away before that."

"The end of the week then. In Albany. Make it Saturday. I'll register at the Ten Eyck Hotel under the name of Mr. and Mrs.—uh, Lester. Then we're on our way, baby. We're on our way."

"The Ten Eyck in Albany on Saturday. All right."

"Mr. and Mrs. Lester."

"Yes. I'll remember."

"Okay." I raised my hand and the waitress brought me our check, scribbled on it and put it face down on the table. I told Bunny: "We'll drive out there now. Both cars, so you can go straight out to the Fawn Ridge Lodge. But they haven't cleared the snow on the ski slope road, so I'll have to pick you up along the way. There's a roadhouse just before the turn off, on the left side of the highway. I'll meet you there."

I paid the check while Bunny went outside. I watched her walk in that tight, controlled, provocative stride she had, her beautiful legs sheathed in those nylon stretch ski pants showing just the slightest suggestion of hip swing. It was sex at its unself-conscious best, and other girls doing a bump-and-grind to seductive music in a pink spotlight couldn't have gotten the idea across half so well.

After the door shut behind her I left half a dollar on the table, got up and went outside. As I climbed into the station wagon in the Marcy parking lot, I saw Bunny swinging out in the gray sedan between the snow banks that flanked the entrance. I gave her a few more seconds and started driving. A few minutes later I drove up in front of the roadhouse on Route 86 and saw Bunny coming out of her car. Then she was sitting alongside of me and I started driving again.

"Watch where you're driving, Chuck. You'll make me blush."

"Did anyone ever tell you you have a really terrific walk?"

"I practice it in my spare time."

"No. That's what I mean. It's the most natural thing in the world."

We parked in front of the ski lodge and went inside

together. I was conscious of Bunny's fast, shallow breathing as I unlocked the supply room door. Then we were standing together over the gladstone bag.

"Open it," Bunny urged me in a very small voice. "Open it, Chuck."

I opened the bag, hearing that fast, shallow breathing close to my ear and feeling her weight on my shoulder as she leaned over me. Then her weight shifted and I thought she was going to bend down over the money. Instead, her fingers touched my neck lightly and her hand rested on my cheek, pulling my head around gently. Still squatting on my hams, I started to turn. She had gone down to her knees. She drew my head against her breast and held it there. I could hear the beating of her heart. After a while I pulled back a little and looked up at those depthless husky eyes so close above my own. They seemed to grow. Big and so close I couldn't focus on them and luminous, they became the whole world. I pulled her head down and kissed her.

Her lips were warm and soft, and when they parted for me the money that was here in the room with us could have been a million miles away. The first time here in the lodge with her it had been all sculpture and motion, the breathtaking awareness of every curve of her body and every movement we shared. But now, this time, it was more like music with the form and the motion merged, and we rose up in the surging rhythm of it to where the rest of the world couldn't reach us. The first time it was graphic and carnal, but beautiful. The first time it was swift. This time it built slowly, and it was sublime.

Afterwards we lay side by side on the bare floor, our flanks touching. Far away I heard a train whistle, its retreating pitch echoing and re-echoing in the mountains.

"I love you," I said. "I never knew I could love anybody the way I love you."

"What I said before, Chuck. You can make me blush. You know, I haven't blushed since I was a little girl, till now. I—I guess I try to keep what I feel inside. All bottled up. But now I like it when you make me blush. When you look at me that way you have."

"I'll make you blush twice a day the rest of our lives."

I leaned on one elbow and kissed her gently on the lips. Then I kissed her eyes, and there was salt on my lips.

"Chuck. Oh, Chuck." She was crying suddenly. "I try to tell myself it isn't right us being so happy like this, after everything that happened. After everything we did. But how can I help being happy—with you?"

"Everything we did we did for each other." I kissed her bruised cheek and tasted the tears there.

Then she said something I would remember all the rest of my life. Sometimes I wish she hadn't said it, but sometimes in a way I know those were the truest, finest words I ever heard. That's when it hurts the most. She said, "I wish ... I wish we'd met long ago, before—Orin. Before the money. Before everything. I wish there was no such thing as the money."

We shared a cigarette, not talking. Then Bunny got up and waited in the big main room of the lodge while I counted six hundred dollars in tens and twenties out of the fortune in the gladstone bag. Most of the bills were creased and rumpled, and I had to smooth them. I shut the bag, snapped it and fastened the straps. Bunny didn't want to watch me. She didn't want to watch any of it.

I gave her the six hundred dollars and she put it in the zipper pocket of her ski jacket, not even looking at it. "Even an hour ago," she said, "in the restaurant, waiting for you and wanting to see you and then having you with me, I still thought the money was the most important thing in the world. Nothing else mattered. Not even how I felt about you. But now, you want to hear something funny? I hate it. I hate the money."

"You're all mixed up," I said quietly but a little desperately. "Your husband and the inquest and what you still have to do."

"Oh, don't worry. I want what the money can do for us. But I hate it. I'll always hate it and hate the need for wanting it. I can't help that."

We drove back to the roadhouse with the gladstone bag in the back of the station wagon. I didn't transfer it to Bunny's car there. Instead, we drove the car and the station wagon a few hundred yards down the road and parked, and when there was no traffic in either direction I got out of the station wagon quickly while she opened the trunk of her car quickly and in a moment the gladstone bag was inside there and I pulled the lid down and she locked it.

"Don't forget at the inquest," I said. "We hardly know each other. Keep it that way."

"Yes, I know."

"After that I'll see you in Albany. But until the inquest, don't leave the Fawn Ridge Lodge unless you have to. It's the only place on that stretch of road up to Saranac Lake and no one will bother you."

"Yes, all right."

"After that, you clear up what you have to in the city and I'll meet you in Albany."

"In Albany," Bunny said, looking up at me with the wind blowing her blond hair and the snow-reflected sun making her eyes seem paler than they were.

"We're on our way." It was a faintly bitter echo of the words I had spoken earlier.

CHAPTER TWENTY

Just before noon on Tuesday, Joe Moon got in touch with me. I'd spent Monday afternoon at the ski slopes with Danny Giardello, working on the tow trails and finally, just before darkness, trying them out. There were a couple of rough spots where you had to ease up on the cable or risk a broken leg, but Danny could smooth them out in the morning, I thought.

Monday night I'd wandered about the hotel public rooms with a frozen grin and forced chatter and a little too much to drink, signing up the skiers for Tuesday's classes. I couldn't get Bunny out of my mind. A gesture, a word, a girl's smile, and I was back there with her again at the lodge, kissing her tears away and seeing the change in her and feeling the hurt she had felt and not being able to help her. Then, later that night in bed, staring up at the darkness because I couldn't fall asleep, I even had a crazy notion to leave the money in Albany and maybe call the police anonymously and tell them what money it was. But it was crazy, all right—we had killed for the money, and we were going to have to live with that no matter what we did. Besides, I wanted it, didn't I? All along I'd wanted it. Then what the hell was the matter with me?

Tuesday morning Inez and Kirby Rowe were huddled over their breakfast, talking earnestly. When they saw me across the dining room they broke it off for a while self-consciously, but then started up again.

Just before I finished my coffee, a man I had never

seen before joined Kirby and Inez at their table. He was thin and middle-aged, with the kind of nondescript, vaguely hangdog face you'd find on any crowded street in any city in the country. From where I sat I could see Kirby making the introductions. Inez smiled a little nervously, I thought, then they all started talking. After a while I got tired of watching them, put on my ski jacket and went outside to find Danny Giardello.

He had a pleased smile on his face that widened to a grin when he saw me. "They're not suspicious of me anymore," he said, meaning the huskies. "Another couple of days like this and I'll be able to harness them and take the sleds out."

"That's swell, Danny. When do you feed them?"

"About four-thirty."

"Well, listen. I'm probably going to be called for that inquest some time today, so how would you like to take the skiing classes out in the bus?"

Danny went on grinning. He liked to ski as much as I did. "I'd like that, sure."

I gave him the lists of beginning and intermediate skiers and went through the series of lessons I wanted them given. "Can you handle it?"

"Don't worry," he said. "I eat that stuff up."

I hung around outside a few minutes watching the skiers assemble. One of the last to arrive was the middle-aged guy that Kirby Rowe had introduced to Inez. He wore a beginner's tag and carried his rented skis from the garage awkwardly, cradling them in both arms and banging the trailing ends against the side of the bus. Since I hadn't signed him up last night, I figured Elaine Skinner had made out his tag for him.

After the bus was loaded, I headed for the front

entrance of the hotel. Then I heard a clattering sound behind me. When I turned around I saw the middle-aged guy getting off the bus banging his skis again. I went over and showed him how to carry them over his shoulder, with the baskets of the poles crossing behind his neck and locking the skis so they wouldn't shift around.

"That's all right," he said. "I'm sure it's just what I ought to do if I was going out there." He shook his head, smiling deprecatingly. "But I kind of chickened out, I guess. I'm at no age to start fooling around with these lethal weapons."

I shrugged and told him Elaine Skinner would give him a refund if he'd already paid for the lessons. Nodding and carrying the skis on his shoulder the way I'd showed him, he returned to the garage. It struck me a little odd at first, but then the bus pulled out with a groaning roar from its exhaust, Danny waved and I went inside forgetting about the little man who'd decided not to ski. It was a free country, wasn't it?

I hung around a couple of hours, chewing the rag with Elaine and Sammy and getting into a long conversation about slalom competition with an intermediate skier who had sprained his ankle last week. After that, Kirby called me to the desk where a call was waiting for me. I nodded to the PBX girl through the open doorway and she pointed to one the house phones.

"Odlum speaking," I said into it.

"This is Joe Moon, Chuck," the deputy's loud voice boomed in my ear. "They're holding that inquest at the municipal building in Wilmington at three o'clock."

"I'll be there. Thanks." I swallowed twice. My mouth was dry and I thought: this is it, the last detail, then nothing else between you and Bunny. And a hundred and seventeen thousand bucks.

"I'll be driving up to Wilmington myself," Joe Moon boomed. "You didn't think I'd miss the inquest, did you?" He laughed good-naturedly. "Shoot, some law officers chase fire engines. Me, I drop in on every inquest in the county. Want me to pick you up?"

I liked the idea right away. If anything was going on that I should know about, talkative, pink-cheeked Joe Moon was the man to see. "Thanks a lot, Joe," I said. "I'd appreciate that. What time?"

"Say two-twenty. I'll drop by the hotel. Give us plenty of time to get down there."

"Right, I'll be ready."

"See you later then."

"So long."

I hung up thinking, not quite three hours to wait, and Bunny had been waiting, alone at the Fawn Ridge Lodge, twenty-four hours now. No, not quite that long, for first she'd paid her bill at the hospital and paid the undertaker. Well, it wouldn't be much longer for both of us. The waiting was hell. It was the waiting which had given both of us doubts about the money. Once we started moving, things would change.

I had an early lunch and saw the bus return from the ski slopes. Danny jawed with me a while about how well it had gone. They were just words, and I could hardly follow them. All during the early afternoon the tension built in me, ready to explode.

When Joe Moon drove up in the gray sheriff's car with the black lettering on the door I was already waiting outside. I waved and he pulled up, stepping on the gas with the gears in neutral to keep the engine idling smoothly. He wasn't wearing a hat. He never wore one, in any kind of weather. His thin corn silk hair was combed neatly over his pink scalp and his plump pink cheeks glowed as if he'd spent the morning scrubbing them. His lips were set, but a smile threatened to break out of his mild blue eyes and all over his face.

"Hop in," he said, and the smile broke. "Smoke?"

I nodded, and we lit up as he started driving. "Boy," he told me, "have I got a story."

"The dogs?"

"You think I'd be grinning like this if it was them polar bears of yours? No, the vet figures those that haven't turned up so far have more'n likely starved to death. We'll worry about them dogs when they start stinking up the landscape in the spring thaws. This is different." He chuckled, waiting for a reaction. But I didn't have any. All I could do was sit there wondering what he was driving at. He relished that. A lawman who never had anything more important to worry about than some stray dogs or a summons to serve, he loved to talk about his work, to dramatize it.

"I wish I was younger," he said finally. "Know what I'd do? I'd finish up two years of college and put in for the FBI. There's a bunch that don't waste any time, boy. I mean, when they're ready to move they don't just move, they jump—with both feet on your, what's it? solar plexus."

"The FBI?" I repeated blankly. We swung out to pass a big trailer truck with eight or nine small state license plates in back. The day was clear and cold, but the sun hid behind a patch of high clouds. It came out suddenly, glaring on the snow.

"Sun glasses," Joe Moon said. "In the glove compartment."

I jabbed at the lock button and the glove compartment lid popped open. In it there was an old pair of stained pigskin driving gloves, a couple of pencil stubs, a notebook, a flashlight, a pair of handcuffs Joe Moon had probably never had the chance to use and sun glasses in a leather case. I took the glasses out and passed them to him and watched him put them on. When they hid his mild blue eyes with the laughter wrinkles radiating out from the corners, he looked a lot more tough and efficient.

"There ought to be a law," he said. "Man shouldn't be allowed to drive up in these here mountains in the winter without sun glasses. Sun glaring on the snow like that can give you a heap of trouble. Why, I …"

He went on for a while, describing the heap of trouble. What had he said about the FBI? Nothing really. Just that he'd wished he'd joined them and when they moved they didn't just move, they jumped. It didn't have to mean a thing but I couldn't let go of it.

"The FBI's got nothing for you," I said, trying to steer him back to it. "At least you're your own boss."

"When the sheriff don't decide to come down from the county seat."

"That's true."

We started climbing along the mountain road toward Wilmington with the bare slope of Whiteface Mountain dominating the skyline to our left. A bright red sports car with two pairs of skis mounted on top sped by in the other direction.

"Well brother," Joe Moon said at last, "I saw them jump. This morning."

I was aware of my breath coming shallowly, the way it did before the Adirondacks slalom competitions I'd entered the past few years. "Who? The FBI?"

"Sure. The G-Men. That's who I been talking about, ain't it? A whole squad of 'em jumped on Lake Placid this morning, like vultures on the carcass of a dead cow. Must be pretty near the whole damned Adirondacks field office staff from Plattsburg."

"You mean in Lake Placid? Right now?" I asked stupidly.

"Of course I mean in Lake Placid right now."

"What's the matter, did somebody rob the Trust Company?" I said, managing a smile.

"No, but somebody made a deposit there. In the Trust Company. They don't know who yet, but they're narrowing it down. They'll weed it out. Maybe they already have. They just won't go home tonight till they find it, Groff says."

"Who?"

"Groff Tish, he's the chief cashier at the Trust Company. Got the reddest face I ever saw, on account of he didn't discover it himself. Assistant cashier name of Bill Rawley did." Joe Moon shook his head. "Stolen money, Chuck. Hot money. Marked money, how do you like that?"

I felt sick. I wanted to get out of the car and run. If marked money had been deposited at Lake Placid's one bank yesterday, it didn't take much to figure it had come in with either the Mirror Lake Memorial Hospital receipts or from the undertaker who was putting Orin Kemp's body in a casket. No, I thought desperately, not the undertaker—chances were he wouldn't make a Monday deposit. That left the hospital. But either way, it could mean only one thing. Norstad never had told Orin Kemp and Bunny a cock-and-bull story. As a cop he'd been in a position to know, and he'd told them only the truth. The ransom money was hot, it was marked, and Bunny had used it yesterday to tie a noose around her own neck.

"... this here Rawley guy," Joe Moon was saying.

"With Groff Tish and the rest of them it's a business, but with Rawley it's a hobby. Don't ask me how the money was marked or why it was marked, 'cause that I don't know. But Bill Rawley found it, and the G-Men jumped. You should have seen this Rawley, him smiling like the cat that...."

How long? I thought while the booming voice rambled on. How long would it take them to narrow it down to the hospital deposit? Monday was a slow day at the bank. Chances were the only major deposit had come from the hospital. And once they narrowed it down to the hospital and saw Bunny's name on the list of paid bills they'd swarm all over her like maggots.

She didn't know, of course. That was the worst part of it. She had no way of knowing and I had no way of telling her until after the inquest. Right now she was probably in Wilmington, in the red-brick municipal building, exchanging a few sad words with Orin Kemp's brother maybe, and never dreaming the FBI was closing in on her, never dreaming—

That was when it hit me like the shock of cold water in the face. The money wasn't a dream now that could make us forget what we had to do to get it. The money was a millstone. We'd have to leave it and run, because no matter what we did they'd trace it to Bunny. We'd have to run and keep on running until we fell and keep on falling until we could close a black hole over us.

Run?

Sitting through the inquest, through what might be long hours of testimony, while the G-Men with their accountants' brains sifted through the hospital receipts and stumbled over the one name that would make them drop their adding machines and reach for their guns? And all the while Bunny saying whatever she had planned to say and looking properly sorrowful, not knowing that any minute the doors might open and the G-Men come in with their briefcases and their absolutely deadly efficiency and walk up front to where she sat testifying and tell her she was under arrest....

"What's the matter with you, Chuck? You look sick. You coming down with something?"

I felt feverish. Just walk in there to the inquest and sit by quietly while they took her? Or run now, while I still had the chance?

But maybe, I thought wildly, they wouldn't narrow it down to the hospital until later. Maybe we'd have time, at least enough time to start running together.

"What's the matter, boy?" Joe Moon asked again.

"Nothing," I mumbled. "It's nothing."

A while later we drove down out of the mountains and along Wilmington's main street. Joe Moon pulled up in front of the municipal building and opened the door. He breathed deeply of the clear cold air.

"Gorgeous day, ain't it?" he said.

I followed him up the stairs and inside.

I saw bright sunshine, dazzling on the snow. I saw a thick dark hedge of yew mantled with snow. I saw the red-brick facade of the building and some motto or other inscribed over the doorway.

Except for my head I felt numb all over. The top of my head felt ready to burst open.

CHAPTER TWENTY-ONE

We were the last ones to show up for the inquest except for the G-men, if they were coming.

They held the inquest in a large basement room with a couple of dozen folding chairs opened for the occasion. Banks of fluorescent lights on the ceiling cast a harsh white glare. The walls of the room had been freshly painted a pale yellow; you could still smell the paint. Up front, near an American flag and the state flag of New York, there was a big desk and behind it sat the coroner, a relaxed little man smoking a pipe. Near him was a stiff-backed chair that would be for the witnesses. It had rectangular wooden arm rests stained almost black from all the hands that had gripped them, waiting for the questions. About ten feet from the witness chair sat the coroner's jury in two neat rows. I looked them over as I was ushered by a uniformed policeman to a seat in the front row of folding chairs. They seemed as relaxed as the pipe-smoking coroner. After all, only a technicality of law had brought them here, for Orin Kemp's death from exposure would go down in the books as an accident, the coroner knew it and looking at the coroner, they probably knew it too.

I heard a chair scrape behind me and knew that Joe Moon had taken his seat. The way the folding chairs were arranged, my back was to the door. If the G-Men came in, I wouldn't see them until they moved down the aisle and were almost on top of me. I shuddered and looked around while the coroner banged the dottle out of his pipe and shuffled some papers on his desk. What was the matter with him? I thought. Wasn't he ever going to get started? There was a big clock on the wall behind his desk. Five after three, and then the minute hand jerked forward the way they do on some of those big electric clocks, biting off and swallowing two minutes of time.

I felt a hand on my arm. It was Sergeant Walters, seated in the next chair. He looked neat and very professional in his state trooper's grays, and he nodded and smiled at me. I managed a smile in return, and looked beyond him. The old man from the Esso station sat to his left, wearing a tie and poking a finger in his stiff white collar. Beyond him sat the doctor—what was his name? Holland—from the Mirror Lake Memorial Hospital. To his left was a tall slender man I'd never seen before, Orin Kemp's brother probably, in a dark blue suit and a black tie. And seated next to him, at the very end of the row in a gray dress with a black mourning band on the sleeve was Bunny. I took one look and tore my eyes away from her. I didn't want to be caught staring at her. We hardly knew each other, that was the plan, and that was the way it would stay.

The coroner stuck one of those little metal cleaning gadgets in his pipe and got out a lump of moist dottle. He cleared his throat. I shot a glance at the clock. The minute hand had bitten off two more two-minute stretches of time. Eleven after three. The coroner dropped his pipe in the pocket of his tweed jacket. I shifted my feet and crossed my legs and then uncrossed them. A bus or a truck rumbled by outside. It was warm in there. I unzippered my ski jacket and mopped sweat off my forehead with a handkerchief. I looked at Bunny again. Her hands were folded in her lap. Orin Kemp's brother, next to her, was staring straight ahead. My head was pounding, a sickening throb in time to my pulse beat. I had a crazy thought—can't they hear it, can't they all hear it?

Then the coroner began to talk. He had a raspy whine of a voice that cut into my jangled nerves like a bin saw. As the law required in accidents of this kind, he had performed an autopsy on the body of the deceased, he said. The cause of death had been fulminating pneumonia, with the entire right lung and most of the left lung affected. Other injuries, which had indirectly caused his exposure, were a simple fracture of the right tibia and a severely sprained left ankle.

The door behind me opened, and I held my breath. I heard footsteps coming down the narrow aisle between the folding chairs. A uniformed figure came into view, put a paper on the coroner's desk and went back out. The coroner nodded, looked at the paper, and muttered something about a negative lab report on the contents of the deceased's stomach. My head pounded and pounded.

The first one they called was Dr. Holland, who quickly established that the coroner's findings coincided with the hospital's. The coroner thanked him, and he went back to his folding chair. It was then almost three-thirty.

Sergeant Walters was next. My palms were damp with sweat and my head went on throbbing. I could hardly follow his testimony—it was something about answering Mr. Heinlein's call at the gas station and finding the body after the injured woman—he identified her as Mrs. Kemp—had cried out something about her husband.

Then Heinlein, looking ridiculous in khaki pants, a blue serge double-breasted jacket and the too-tight tie and collar, took the witness chair. He smiled self-consciously but happily too, basking in the limelight. I'll never forget how he kept running his finger around under his collar. He took his time about everything, rambling on and on. He told them the story he had told me, about the body he had found twenty-five years ago. "Damn near killed the old lady, when the *po*-lice called her and said, either your husband kilt a man or he's lyin' there dead on the road...." They asked him about the gasoline can. Earlier, he had identified Orin Kemp as the man who had borrowed it, and now he testified to this before the coroner's jury. He told us about the storm. Everyone in this room had been through it, but there was no shutting him up. I looked at the clock, and at his finger that tugged and tugged under the stiff collar. I wanted to get up and hit him. "Usta snow like that every year two three times, but lately ... winters ain't what they used to be ... in my time ... fellow ought to watch the gas gauge more careful-like ... fifty-three inches, the paper said, but down by the station I had sixty inches if it was foot...."

Had they narrowed it down to the hospital now? Had they found Bunny's name on her paid bill? Were they on their way to Wilmington through the glare of sun on snow? Or maybe they'd call. Just a simple phone call, and Bunny wouldn't leave this building until they got here, when she'd leave in their custody.

"Mr. Charles Odlum."

They had to repeat it twice. Walters nudged me, and I blinked and saw the witness chair was empty. I sat down in it. I looked at Bunny. Joe Moon, sitting in the second row, caught my eye. He winked.

My part was simple, but I was conscious of time standing still, just standing still and waiting for them. You found the woman out there in the snow off Route 86, Mr. Odlum? Yes, I did. Will you tell the coroner's jury about it? I told them. And you saw no sign of her husband, of the deceased? No. Or the dog? No. Then I told them about Lester and Helen, who were in Canada now and hadn't been sent for. Until you reached the gas station, did the woman say anything about her husband? No, she was in no condition to say anything.

Then I was sitting down again next to Walters.

"Mrs. Bonita Kemp."

Her brother-in-law went with her to the witness chair. She leaned on his arm a little. Their mutual grief was almost like a physical thing you could touch. Bunny was magnificent, but what good would it do her if the Feds showed up in the middle of it? And she didn't know about the money, I kept telling myself. She had no way of knowing. If they came, and if they socked it to her suddenly, she might come all unstrung. She might blurt the whole thing out.

"I'm sorry we have to put you through this ordeal," the coroner said, "but we'll try to be as brief as possible, Mrs. Kemp. Your car stopped. The gas tank was empty, as has since been verified. Then what happened?"

All the eagerness which I always associated with Bunny's voice was gone. She gave it to them in a flat, listless monotone with plenty of pauses. Every now and then she'd finger the big bandage on her cheek nervously. She'd had a day and a night to rehearse it in, and she didn't miss a trick.

"Well, we had noticed this sign that said a gas station was down the road. Orin ... told me to wait in the car. He went ahead on foot. It was snowing very hard, and after a little while I couldn't see him. I waited and waited. I ... I wanted to go myself because of his ankle, but he wouldn't hear of it. He didn't come back in half an hour. I began to get worried. I thought maybe the ankle had given under him and he was hurt. I got out of the car to look for him. Then I heard this howling and ... and...." Her voice broke. A uniformed cop gave her a drink of water from the pitcher that was on the coroner's desk.

"I'm sorry," she said after taking a sip. "I saw this dog. Just standing there in the snow, looking at me. I had walked down the road a little, looking for ... Orin.

I got scared I started running. Maybe if I had tried to make it back to the car I would have been all right. Maybe if I just stood still, but I ..."

"That's all right, Mrs. Kemp," the coroner said. "We understand."

"Well, I started running up the hill. I heard the dog yelping behind me. I ran and I ... then I turned around and it leaped at me. My face, it ... I screamed. I could smell it, the dog. I screamed and I ... I must have fainted. The next thing I remember, I was in the gas station and...."

"That ought to be enough, Mrs. Kemp," the coroner said "You've been very patient with us."

The brother-in-law helped her back to her seat. Then the coroner spoke to the jury for a few minutes. I couldn't keep to his train of thought. It was almost four o'clock. I blinked because sweat ran into my eye. I took my ski jacket off and folded it on my lap. I heard chairs scraping as the coroner's jury huddled. The minute hand jumped again. Four o'clock. The chairs scraped once more and the jury foreman was busy writing for a few minutes. All the other jurymen crowded around, looking at what he was writing, glancing at one another and nodding. Then the foreman brought what he had written over to the coroner, who read it, mumbled, "Thank you, Matt," cleared his throat and read:

"It is the verdict of this jury that the deceased, Orin Kemp, met his death by accidental exposure to the elements on...."

That was it, the last detail, and now it didn't mean a thing. I looked at Bunny. She was staring down at her hands clasped in her lap and I knew what she thought: we were home free. I wanted to shout the truth to her, but all I could do was nod when chairs started to scrape and Sergeant Walters said something to me.

I got up. I started to walk toward the back of the room. Once I turned around. Bunny and her brother-in-law were talking to the coroner who was stuffing tobacco in his pipe. I went upstairs and outside, waiting on the steps for Joe Moon. The late afternoon sun cast long shadows and a cold wind blew little flurries off the snow drifts. Would I get a chance to talk to her?

They began to come out then. The members of the jury first, then two uniformed cops, then a few people I didn't recognize. I lit a cigarette and heard cars start up in the parking lot. Maybe they'd come now, I thought bitterly, after the verdict had given Bunny her moment of triumph. Or maybe, inside, they had just now called. Maybe that was why Bunny hadn't come out yet. I threw the cigarette away and lit another one. It didn't taste any better. My hands were shaking.

Then she was on the steps beside me with her brother-in-law and the coroner. I heard her say: "No, it's all right, Tom. You go ahead and straighten out the details. I'm tired. I just don't want to talk anymore. About anything."

He squeezed her hand. "I'll be leaving with the ... on the train first thing in the morning. You sure you'll be okay driving down alone?"

"I'd rather, Tom. Honest, I'd rather."

He kissed her cheek and the coroner shook her hand and she started down the steps. "Mrs. Kemp," I called.

The two men looked at me and Bunny turned around slowly, squinting in the afternoon sunlight. "Oh, Mr. Odlum," she said. "I never did get to thank you for what you did."

They were watching us. "It's nothing any man wouldn't have done in my place, Mrs. Kemp." Run, I thought. We've got to run. Can't you see it in my face?

It would only take a few seconds to tell her. I fell into step with her at the bottom of the flight of stairs, but they were still within earshot. We started walking along the path to the parking lot.

"Hey, Chuck. Wait up a minute."

I turned around. It was Joe Moon coming down the stairs. I could feel the hopeless frustration holding me and shaking me. I thrust my hands in the pockets of my ski pants because they were trembling so. We waited for Joe Moon, then the three of us walked to her gray sedan that still had snow on the roof. She shook my hand coolly and said something. Maybe she could feel it shake, I thought. But so what? Of course I'd be tense.

She got in behind the wheel. Joe Moon said something. I said something. She started to drive. She doesn't know, I thought. You haven't told her. She'll go back there to the Fawn Ridge Lodge, to the hundred and seventeen thousand bucks. The police will know where, because she had to tell them where she was staying for the inquest. She'll go back there and just wait.

Until they came for her in unmarked cars, with no sirens screaming, with no warning until the hard hand closed on her arm.

Mighty convenient, Mrs. Kemp, your husband dying and you with all that money.

I watched her turn at the exit of the parking lot and drive away. A few other cars pulled out.

"... wet your whistle?" Joe Moon asked.

"What? What did you say?"

"Want to have a couple of beers before we start

back?"

"Well, I've got things to do at the hotel."

"Just one beer then. Come on."

I walked with him on lead feet out of the parking lot and across the street. We went into a bar and grill and sat down at the bar and then there was a glass of beer in my hand and I was drinking it. Joe Moon began to yammer. Every now and then I nodded. I didn't hear a word he said.

At twenty to five we went back outside. My head was pounding fiercely. Twenty minutes, I thought. She'd been on her way in twenty minutes.

Joe Moon wasn't in any hurry. He kept it down around thirty-five on the flat stretches, and most of the way was up hill and down and around sharp switchbacks. It took us almost forty minutes to reach Lake Placid and another five to get to Mirror Lake. Dusk was settling, giving the snow that bluish quality it gets in the mountains just before darkness.

"... speed limit on the Thruway," Joe Moon said as he pulled up in front of the hotel. He hadn't stopped talking all the way back.

"Well, thanks, Joe."

"Shoot, you're a good listener, boy."

I opened the door.

"I wonder if they got to it yet."

"Who?"

"The G-Men. They will, brother. You can bank on that. They will." Joe Moon smiled his appreciation of the FBI. "They always do. Well, see you."

He waved and drove off.

I took a deep breath and went around back and inside through the kitchen entrance. I had a bag packed and ready to go and it had seemed silly when I did it, but now I needed it, for we didn't have any money to buy clothes and I'd be easy to spot in a ski outfit once we got out of the skiing country. If we got out, I thought. If they didn't get to her first.

I went upstairs and got my bag and started down again. Less than thirty bucks in my pocket, I thought. Not much of a lamming fund for two fugitives, but if Bunny hadn't spent all of the seventy dollars Orin Kemp had had on him when he died, that would give us a little more.

On the stairs I passed someone. The little guy with the hang-dog look. He was wearing a turtleneck sweater and a leather windbreaker, unzippered, over it. He nodded at me and kept going up.

The only vehicle I had the keys to was the station wagon. I didn't like that, because if I left it at the Fawn Ridge Lodge they'd know right away I'd run off with Bunny and they'd know who they had to look for. Maybe, I thought, we could leave in both cars and ditch the station wagon somewhere. Cross that bridge when you reach it.

But hurry. Just hurry.

I got into the station wagon and fumbled with the keys. It was almost dark now. I started the wagon, backed out of the parking slot and swung west on Route 86. It was eight miles to the Fawn Ridge Lodge, and I really gunned it. There were patches of ice on the road, but most of it was straight and flat and I had four-wheel-drive. I kept the throttle to the floorboards. The steering wheel bounced and shook like something alive in my hands. I watched the speedometer needle climb, wobbling, to seventy. I watched the twin tunnels of the headlights eat up distance and time. I felt cold all over, but I was sweating. What if they'd already got to her?

It took me eight minutes to go those eight miles.

You could see the Fawn Ridge Lodge from a long way off even at night, for bright floodlights on posts lit the parking field and the windows of the restaurant in the main building were brightly lighted too. Beyond the parking field were the separate cabins of the lodge, eight of them with their rears to a frozen stream and the split logs of their fronts looking black in the light of the parking field.

A few cars were parked in front of the restaurant, but most of the cabins were dark and deserted. The one nearest the restaurant had a car in front of it, a convertible.

I saw her car parked at the edge of the parking field in front of the last cabin in line.

I pulled up alongside it and was running as soon as my ski boots hit the packed snow of the parking field. Each cabin had its own stand of white birch out front, so you had to park a little ways off and under the lights. There was a small porch and a light in the window behind it. I ran up on the porch and knocked on the door, not even thinking that they might be here already.

After a while I heard her footsteps inside. "Yes? Who is it?"

"Chuck. Open up. Hurry."

The door swung in and I saw her. She was wearing a flannel bathrobe. Her legs were bare under it and she was barefoot. She'd have to dress.

I shut the door and leaned on it.

"What's the matter with you? You know you shouldn't have come here."

"Get dressed," I said, panting. "Where's your bag. I'll pack."

She just stood there, looking at me, those astonishing eyes wide and uncomprehending. I was wild with the waiting and the reckless drive and not knowing if they'd come for her already. Maybe, in another minute, I'd be coherent. But now I just said: "Move."

She just stood there.

I grabbed her shoulders and shook her. I was like a madman. I wanted to calm down by couldn't, not right away. She struggled to get free of me. I shouted something hoarsely. She brought one of her hands up between us. I shoved forward into the room, wanting to find her bag and start packing. She stumbled and clutched out. I felt her fingernails rake my cheek and I let go of her and stepped back.

"God, Chuck. I'm sorry. I didn't mean to. You're bleeding." I took my handkerchief out and dabbed at the scratches on my cheek. My head was hammering, but I took a deep breath and gave it to her: "Listen. The FBI. They're in town. The money's marked. I don't know how. They're tracing it. From the hospital bank deposit. The cops know where you are. As soon as they see your name the G-men will be here. Maybe they're on their way now. Maybe they're going to put up road blocks. There aren't many roads out of these mountains. Get dressed. I'll pack. We've got to hurry."

She never questioned it. Not the way I was. She went over between the twin beds that took up most of the small room and stood there a minute looking at me. She pulled the gladstone bag out from under one of the beds, unbuckled the straps and opened it.

"Look," she said. "Look at it." Tears glistened in her eyes. "You want to know something?"

I thought she'd be getting her own suitcase out. "For crying out loud," I said, "no postmortems."

"You want to know something?" she repeated, ignoring that. "It got so I couldn't look at it. All day yesterday and this morning. The money, right here in this room with me. I just couldn't look at it. I hated it. I was sick with the idea of it. I ... you want to know something, Chuck? I'm glad. I'm glad. I never could have—"

"Save it," I snapped at her. "Tell me how glad you are we get out of this."

She went to the closet and took her suitcase out. I opened it for her on one of the beds and started to empty the contents of the dresser drawers into it. On my second go at the dresser I bumped into her. She had taken the flannel robe off and stood there in her slip that clung to the curves of her body. Then I took her into my arms, just for a minute, and she was crying. "Oh, Chuck, Chuck, don't you see? With us the money came later. You didn't even know about it until later, until after ..."

"All right," I said, stroking her blond hair. "It's going to be all right." I tilted her chin up and kissed her tears, the way I had in the ski lodge.

"I love you," she said. "I think I never knew how much, not really how much, till now. In the beginning, with Jack McCall, it wasn't like that. He ... he was going to help me with the money. He wanted it, but he was scared too and I didn't—"

"Not now," I said, coming out of it. "Just hurry. For Christ's sake, hurry."

She took the gray dress out of the closet and laid it out on the bed. While I threw the rest of her stuff from the closet into her suitcase, she sat down on the edge of the bed with a pair of wispy nylons. I snapped the bag shut and headed for the door with it.

"Where are you going?"

"Give me the keys, I'll warm your car."

"I was just driving," she said, molding one of the nylons to her leg. "You don't have to warm it."

"All right. All right. I'll wait outside in the station wagon. Maybe if we're lucky no one will see us together. We'll drive back down to Mirror Lake and leave the station wagon there and I'll get in the car. Then they'll be looking for you. They won't be looking for two of us together. We'll have a chance that way."

"Mirror Lake? But if the police—"

"We've got to. The all-weather road stops at Saranac Lake the other way. We've got to go back."

"I'll be out in five minutes."

I opened the door and went outside with her suitcase. I went across the porch. Through the clump of white birch I could see her car and the station wagon, with *Whiteface Hotel* stenciled on its side, in the brightly lit parking lot. I took a step down off the porch and thought about the money. What was the matter with me? Leave it here? Then they'd know for sure. Otherwise they'd have a guess, a very good guess under the circumstances, but nothing they could prove. Take the money with us? It was a chance, because we might be caught with it. But being caught with it was no worse than leaving it in the cabin she'd rented.

That's it, I thought. That's it. Take it away with you and get rid of it somewhere.

I turned around with her suitcase in my hand.

Something rustled among the birches.

I started to swing back toward the sound. From the corner of my eye I saw a figure looming in the darkness between the porch and the clump of birch.

Then my head split and the night rushed in and I was falling through the night and the snow at my feet seemed miles away.

CHAPTER TWENTY-TWO

I got to my hands and knees in time to see him coming out of the cabin.

The light from the open door was behind him. He was carrying the gladstone.

Norstad.

He reached me on the run, lugging the heavy gladstone, and kicked me. I was still numb. I hardly felt it, but I went over on my back. I heard him running. I started to get up again. Staggered through the birches and across the parking field.

A car swung away from the restaurant. I went toward it, then dived out of the way as it almost ran me down. Picking myself up, I took three strides toward where the station wagon was parked.

Chase him?

What for? Let him have the money. We didn't want it now. We couldn't use it. He had ways he could get rid of it, hadn't Bunny told me that? Maybe he'd get away with it, I thought, but if he did we wouldn't be any worse off. And if he didn't, they'd nab him with the money and we'd be in the clear. He couldn't prove anything about Orin Kemp, and no one would ever learn what had happened to Jack McCall.

I saw the tail lights of his car swing in a slight skid as he turned out of the parking field. I went back to the cabin. The door was open and light streamed out.

"Bunny?" I called softly.

She didn't answer.

I walked across the porch and went inside, pushing the door shut and telling myself we should have figured this was the time Norstad would make his move, for all he had to do was wait at the municipal building in Wilmington and follow her back to the cabin. But why had he waited outside so long? Maybe, I thought, he'd decided to lift the gladstone off her when she came out of the cabin. Maybe he'd been waiting to see what she'd do. Then he'd seen me come, and he'd sapped me and ...

Then I saw her.

She was on her back on the bed with her slip torn and only one of the nylon stockings on her leg. The lamp on the night table was overturned, the throw rug on the floor was crumpled in a corner and the bedspread on the other bed was pulled almost completely off. She had put up a terrific struggle, but it hadn't been enough.

The other nylon stocking was around her neck.

I stood there, feeling the world drop out from under me. I didn't want to look at her, but I couldn't stop. I gagged and retched emptily. Her eyes were wide and swollen almost out of her head, those astonishingly beautiful eyes, those husky eyes which had first attracted me to her, changed finally and for all time. Her tongue was thick and protruding. Her face was a ghastly color.

I went to her. I stood over her and I cried. How long I stood there I don't know. Time stopped and I knew, for me, it would never start again.

I looked at her. In their struggle the bandage had been ripped from her face and the ugly black surgical stitching formed an inverted "V" on her cheek. I couldn't touch her and I didn't even want to stand there looking at her, because she wasn't the same. She wasn't Bunny.

Norstad, I thought. He was waiting outside all the time because he knew he had to kill her, not just take the money but kill her so she couldn't connect him with it. He'd been outside in the darkness, screwing up his courage, waiting. And when I entered the picture, he'd had to act.

One small part of my mind said, you've got to get away. You've got to get away, you can't help her now, she's beyond help, she'd want you to get away. She'd want you to run while you still can.

But I just stood there, looking at her and not wanting to look at her.

Then I heard a car. All right, I thought, give him time to get out and go wherever he's going, the restaurant or one of the cabins, and then run for it. She'd want you to do that.

The car pulled up outside. I heard the door slam. If it was the FBI?

If it was, they'd have me. If it wasn't, I'd run. For Bunny.

I heard footsteps on the porch. Someone pounded at the door.

"Open up in there! I know you're in there, Odlum."

The FBI, I thought, hardly caring. That's it.

Odlum? He had said Odlum. How did they know I was there?

"Come on, Odlum. Open up."

I swung around to face the door. I hadn't locked it. The knob started to turn.

When he came in he was even more surprised than I was. He had expected it to be locked.

Little man with a hang-dog look. Turtleneck sweater with a lumber jacket zippered over it. In a way, it was ludicrous. He had one of those small 35mm cameras in his hand with a flash attachment. He looked at me and looked at the bed and he dropped it. We just stared at each other and I took a step toward him. I wasn't going to do anything, but he couldn't have known that. He clawed at his lumber jacket and then he had a gun in his hand.

"Back up and sit down on the bed, Odlum," he said. His eyes were popping. He could hardly talk.

Then he went to the phone and asked the operator for the police.

They came for me in a little while. They took a lot of pictures and talked to the hang-dog man and he answered them. They asked me questions and they mustn't have liked my answers. They started to shove me around a little and the pain in my head blossomed and I thought of Norstad.

I ran to the door. Faces appeared and I struck out at them and they went away magically but others took their place. I recognized one of them as the face of the state trooper who'd been with Sergeant Walters that day we brought Orin Kemp in. I hit him and he didn't go down.

I made it outside to the porch. I screamed, "He killed her. You've got to stop him. He killed her. He killed her."

Then they fell on me and I went down off the porch into the snow and the shouting voice drifted and softened and went away.

They've got me under this light and they keep throwing questions at me. Sometimes I answer them. The scratches on your cheek. Sure, she scratched me. But we'd never hurt each other. We were in love. Didn't you struggle? Didn't she scratch you, fighting for her life? Isn't that how you hurt your head, struggling with her?

Where's the money, Odlum? Sergeant Walters' voice, bitter.

They'd found some of the money in the gray dress

Bunny was going to wear, money I'd given her at the ski lodge. She hadn't spent all of it. It was just like Sloan and Hannah Howard all over again. I hid the money. They wanted it, and I wouldn't tell them where.

If I'd run right away, I could have had an hour's head start on the FBI, for as it turned out there were some Monday hotel deposits at the bank which hadn't been brought in on Friday because of the storm and they hadn't touched the hospital paid bills till late this afternoon. But I had brought it all tumbling down on me. That got through to me after a while, when the FBI came and started throwing questions at me along with the state police. The little man with the hang-dog face was a private detective up from Albany. Kirby Rowe had hired him, had talked Inez into it. He had his camera and he'd followed me from the hotel. He was going to get the evidence Inez would need for a New York divorce. His name was Sprague, or something like that. He hadn't been able to keep up with the four-wheel-drive station wagon on the icy road between Mirror Lake and the Fawn Ridge Lodge, but he'd seen the wagon under the bright lights of the parking field.

I keep telling them, Norstad. Norstad's the one you want. Norstad killed her. I loved her. I wouldn't have hurt her for anything. Norstad. You've got to believe me. There's still time. He's got the money. He still isn't very far. You can plug up the roads. You can stop him. Get him. Get Norstad. He killed her.

"You killed Mrs. Kemp, Odlum. You killed her for the money, why don't you admit it? You killed her."

They had to stop saying that. Just if they would stop saying that. Anything, if they would stop saying that. They had to believe me. I wouldn't have hurt Bunny for anything. They had to believe it. Kemp, I said, telling them about it. I couldn't see them. The bright light stared at me, hurting my eyes. Jack McCall, I said, telling them about him too. But not my Bunny.

I heard them moving around in the darkness beyond the bright light. Norstad, I thought. He had just waited. He wasn't in any hurry. He just waited for us to drop it in his lap, and then he moved.

Kemp, I said, pleading with them. Kemp and Jack McCall. I admit it. Write it down. I'll sign it. But not Bunny.

Maybe they'll go after Norstad. Maybe they'll plug the roads, if they hurry, and stop him. Maybe out there in the darkness they're already doing it.

But they've got to believe me. She'll know, if they believe me, she'll know I didn't kill her.

Because that's the awful part of it. Why assume Norstad followed her back from the inquest? Didn't that leave a time lag you couldn't really explain? And how would he have known about the inquest? No, he didn't follow her. He didn't have to.

He was at the hotel, like Sprague or whatever his name is.

He followed me. He saw the station wagon in the parking field, like Sprague. He parked near the restaurant and came the rest of the way on foot.

If I hadn't gone to her, she'd still be alive.

Wasn't that the same as killing her?

But I'd had to warn her. She didn't know about the FBI.

If they believe I didn't kill her, she'll know I did what had to be done. I loved her. They've got to believe me.

Because they took away the bright light and I'm sitting alone in darkness.

And, big and luminous like a husky's, I see her eyes.

THE END

Stephen Marlowe was born in New York in 1928 and educated in Virginia. He began his career by writing science-fiction for the pulps under his natal name, Milton Lesser, and various pen names. After army service during the Korean War, he adopted the Marlowe name for his mystery fiction and created his detective Chester Drum in 1955 with *The Second Longest Night*. Having changed his name legally, Stephen Marlowe wandered the world in search of material for his equally peripatetic detective. He was awarded France's Prix Gutenberg du Livre in 1988, and in 1997 the Private Eye Writers of America conferred on him their Life Achievement Award. He and his wife Ann lived in Williamsburg, Virginia, until Marlowe's death on February 22, 2008.

STEPHEN MARLOWE BIBLIOGRAPHY

Chester Drum series:

The Second Longest Night (1955)
Mecca for Murder (1956)
Trouble is My Name (1957)
Killers are My Meat (1957)
Murder is My Dish (1957)
Terror is My Trade (1958)
Violence is My Business (1958)
Homicide is My Game (1959)
Double in Trouble [w/Richard Prather] (1959)
Peril is My Pay (1960)
Death is My Comrade (1960)
Danger is My Line (1960)
Manhunt is My Mission (1961)
Jeopardy is My Job (1962)
Francesca (1963)
Drum Beat—Berlin (1964)
Drum Beat—Dominique (1965)
Drum Beat—Madrid (1966)
Drum Beat—Erica (1967)
Drum Beat—Marianne (1968)
Drum Beat: The Chester Drum Casebook (2003)

Non-Series Novels:

Catch the Brass Ring (1954)
Model for Murder (1955)
Turn Left for Murder (1955)
Dead on Arrival (1956)
Blonde Bait (1959)
Passport to Peril (1959)
The Shining (1963)
The Search for Bruno Heidler (1966)
Come Over, Red Rover (1968)
The Summit (1970)
Colossus (1972)
The Man With No Shadow (1974)
The Cawthorn Journals [aka Too Many Chiefs] (1975)
Translation (1976)
The Valkyrie Encounter (1978)
1956 [aka Deborah's Legacy] (1981)
The Memoirs of Christopher Columbus (1987)
The Lighthouse at the End of the World (1995)
The Death and Life of Miguel de Cervantes (1996)

As Adam Chase (with Paul A. Fairman)

The Golden Ape (1959)

As Andrew Frazer

Find Eileen Hardin—Alive! (1959)
The Fall of Marty Moon (1960)

As Darius John Granger

[various sf stories, 1955-1959]

As Milton Lesser

Earthbound (1952)
The Star Seekers (1953)
Looking Forward [editor] (1953)
Recruit for Andromeda (1959)
Stadium Beyond the Stars (1960)
Spacemen, Go Home (1961)
Secret of the Black Planet (1969)

As Ellery Queen

Dead Man's Tale (1961)

As Jason Ridgway

West Side Jungle (1958)
Adam's Fall (1960)
People in Glass Houses (1961)
Hardly a Man is Now Alive (1962)
The Treasure of the Cosa Nostra (1966)

As S. M. Tenneshaw

[various sf stories, 1948-1957]

As C. H. Thames

Violence is Golden (1956)
Blood of My Brother (1963)

www.ingramcontent.com/pod-product-compliance
Lightning Source LLC
LaVergne TN
LVHW010211070526
838199LV00062B/4530